Stay

Other Bella Books by Valerie Kapp

For a Lifetime

About the Author

Valerie Kapp grew up in Pennsylvania and started her college adventure outside Philadelphia, then onto Minnesota. She attended graduate school in Oregon and finally wound up in Dayton, Ohio, where she has lived for forty-one years. She and her wife of forty years have two dogs, Boston and Ziva. You can find Valerie puzzling, riding her Harley motorcycle, golfing with her wife and friends, playing pickleball, visiting New York City to see Broadway plays, or sharing a meal and laughter every Monday night with friends she calls family.

Stay is her second novel.

Bella Books, Inc.
P.O. Box 10543
Tallahassee, FL 32302

First Edition - 2025

Editor: Cath Walker

ISBN: 978-1-64247-635-4

Acknowledgments

Thank you to Kathy T., Judy S., Sandy C., and Judy L. for being my beta readers for *Stay*.

I also want to thank Cath Walker, the Bella Books editor of my first book, *For a Lifetime*, and the Bella Book family, who shared their expertise and demonstrated patience and guidance for a first-time author.

Dedication

This book is dedicated to my mother, who cherished her family above all and taught me to do the same.

Stay

VALERIE KAPP

BELLA
BOOKS

CHAPTER ONE

2009

I collapsed to my knees and grasped Catherine's hand. My voice shook as I called out her name, tears streaming down my face. Everyone rushed around us, and I felt their panic rising.

Marilyn and Frieda moved to my side, their trembling hands frantically checking for a pulse. "Call 911!" Frieda screamed.

The wail of the siren pierced the air as the ambulance pulled into the driveway. Two EMTs jumped out and assessed Catherine's condition.

Marilyn and Stacy pulled me away, wrapping their arms tightly around me.

We watched silently as the EMTs worked in a blur of motion, their hands flying across the gurney and medical equipment as they attached an IV line on one side, hooked up monitors on the other, and attached defibrillator pads to Catherine's chest. The rhythm of their movements was synchronized in a desperate attempt to save her life. Everyone surrounded me, and with each chest compression, tears dripped onto my shoulder as we silently prayed for any sign that she would be all right.

As Nedra drove us to Dayton's Good Samaritan Hospital, I pried my fingers from Marilyn's. My mind tried to grasp what had happened, and dread washed over me as Nedra uttered, "We're here." My stomach clenched as an icy chill ran down my spine.

I burst through the double doors of the ER, crashing them against the wall and drawing everyone's attention to me. I beelined toward the registration counter, narrowly avoiding colliding with an older man being pushed in a wheelchair. The nurse behind the counter was completely engrossed in her computer, oblivious to me.

"Catherine Wolford was just brought in by ambulance," I said as Marilyn, Stacy, and Cindy caught up and stood beside me.

"Are you family? A sister?" the nurse asked.

"Yes, I'm her family. I'm her partner."

"We need her family contact information."

"I *am* her family." I pinched the bridge of my nose, squeezed my eyes tight, and said through clenched teeth, "Her family has not been in her life for fifteen years."

Cindy touched my shoulder. "We'll provide you with the family contact information. But right now, what information can we give you to help Catherine?"

I took a long, measured breath and forced my jaw to relax. I looked at the nurse and asked in a strained but controlled voice, "What information do you need?"

"Do you have her insurance details? Does she have any allergies? Is she taking any medications?" She shoved a clipboard in my direction. "Here's the form. Can you complete it as much as possible and return it to me? That would help greatly."

I walked to the nearest chair and sank into it with an exhausted huff. I ran my trembling fingers through my hair before inhaling deeply and scribbling responses. Nedra and Frieda joined the others, standing or sitting around me, silently watching as I wrote.

Nedra walked with me to return the clipboard, and I asked, "Please, will you tell us her condition?"

"Again, legally, you are not family. I'm not sure how much information I can give you."

"Excuse me," Nedra said.

"Nedra," I cautioned.

She touched my shoulder. "Let me handle this for you."

My hand shot out and gripped her upper arm, my fingers digging into her skin. My voice caught in my throat as I begged, "Please, don't make this any worse than it is."

Nedra turned to the nurse, inhaled, and explained that the Ohio Department of Health and Human Services was developing hospital guidelines prohibiting sexual orientation and gender-identity discrimination.

"I don't..." the nurse began.

"I believe this hospital is working on their guidelines as we speak."

"I wouldn't know anything about that. Let me ask my supervisor." The nurse rose from her chair and retreated through a door.

I stared at Nedra.

The nurse returned. "My supervisor says I can share information about the patient with you. Medical decisions, though, she'll need to investigate."

I glanced at Nedra. She nodded and said, "Okay, acceptable for now."

"So, what is Catherine's status?" I asked.

"She's still being evaluated. A doctor will come as soon as possible to inform you of her condition."

I thanked the nurse as my heart raced. I shuffled alongside Nedra and Frieda when suddenly, Nedra yanked me back. I sidestepped a mother and her teenage son strolling toward us. Nedra mumbled an apology while Frieda guided me to a chair, her delicate touch calming my frayed nerves.

"Nedra, it's a good thing you volunteer your paralegal services at Equality Ohio," Cindy said.

As Nedra explained the guidelines, I stood and paced around the room, my movements sluggish and labored, as if I were walking through molasses. My throat was dry and tight, and my heart pounded as tears coursed down my cheeks. "Damn it! What the fuck? Catherine, where's Catherine?"

Frieda rushed over to me and placed her arm around my shoulder. "Dayna. Please, let's sit down."

CHAPTER TWO

For the following two hours, we tried to distract ourselves, the air heavy with worry.

I exited into the early evening air, the parking lot lights providing a tiny glimmer of solace to the approaching darkness. I trudged up and down the walkway, chanting, "She has to make it. She has to make it." My mind raced, hoping beyond hope that Catherine would pull through.

I squared my shoulders and pushed open the ER doors, determined to stay focused on the hallway ahead. "Any news?" I asked as I approached my friends.

They shook their heads.

"How can this be happening?" Nedra asked no one in particular. "We were swimming, eating, discussing Catherine and Dayna's commitment ceremony, and having fun together as usual. We hugged Catherine and Dayna goodbye, they took a few steps off the patio, and the next thing we saw was Catherine lying on the ground."

"How can she have had a heart attack?" Cindy asked.

"That's what the EMTs said back at the house. A heart attack," Stacy said.

The digital clock on the waiting room wall ticked away the minutes until two more hours passed in agonizing silence, with no news.

"Did the hospital contact her mom?" I asked Marilyn.

"The last time I asked, the nurse said she left a voice message on her phone."

"Maybe I should call her?"

"Why?" Nedra said. "She's an asshole. She only cares about the money and image."

I touched her arm. "She's still her daughter."

"You're more forgiving than me," Nedra mumbled.

"You want to call her mom?" Frieda asked me.

"No. I'll call her brother. I have his number."

After my call to Catherine's brother, Scott, with whom we reconnected two years ago, I continued to sit or pace with the others.

A half hour later, a gray-haired man in a white doctor's coat, a mask hanging around his neck, entered the ER waiting room, his eyes searching. "Dayna?"

I jumped up, adrenaline coursing through me. Everything was in slow motion as my two long strides brought me close to him. My friend's hands on my shoulders reminded me to stay steady and composed. My body trembled.

"Dayna, I'm Doctor Bradley Morgan, the cardiologist treating Catherine." He paused. "Catherine has had a major heart attack, a STEMI."

"What the hell is that?" Nedra asked.

"An ST-elevation myocardial infarction."

"And that means...?" Marilyn questioned.

My knees weakened, and my chest tightened as fifteen years of memories with the love of my life ran through my mind—memories of our first dance, days spent on the beach, and eating chocolate ice cream as we watched NCIS. How we'd celebrate significant milestones together, and how we had courageously faced challenges hand in hand. I was reminded after our final attempt to locate my birth mother I had begun withdrawing from her. She held me and whispered, "I'm not leaving." She had become more to me than a life partner. She had become my world.

"A STEMI is a severe heart attack where one of the heart's major arteries is blocked, usually a one hundred percent blockage. It can cause extensive damage to a large area of the heart."

Cindy turned to the doctor and with her social worker instincts said, "You're not telling us everything."

His eyes scanned everyone's faces. "We're running more tests to evaluate the full damage to the heart. She arrested three times. On the way to the hospital, the EMTs revived her twice, and we revived her again after she arrived."

"Damn." I rubbed my face. "This can't be happening. I need to see her."

"She's in the CICU, the Cardiac Intensive Care Unit."

"Can I see her?"

"She did regain consciousness for a few seconds after we revived her. She called out your name and said—" The doctor touched my arm.

"She said what?" Marilyn asked.

"She said, 'Dayna, I love you.'"

My hand covered my mouth. "Oh, Catherine."

"For that reason, I am sharing her condition with you. I assume, as you stated at the front desk, you are life partners."

I wiped away tears, straightened my shoulders, and broke free from the tight hold of everyone's embrace. I trembled. "Can I see her now?"

"There's more, right, Doctor?" Cindy asked.

"Jesus Christ, Cindy," Nedra barked. "How can there be more?"

"Yes. You need to prepare for the worst."

"What do you mean?" Marilyn asked, putting her hand around my waist.

"She was immediately rushed to the cath lab and had an emergency angiogram to determine the condition of the coronary arteries. She had nearly total blockage of three of them. We then did an angioplasty procedure to open them. However, Catherine remained unconscious. And as I said, we're running more tests to determine the next step if the angioplasty doesn't work."

"And the worst being?" asked Marilyn.

Doctor Morgan said, "A STEMI heart attack is also called a widow-maker."

I gasped for air as tears blurred my vision, and my friends quickly caught me before I crumpled into a heap on the floor.

Frieda told me, "Breathe, Dayna. Breathe."

Everyone stared at the doctor and then at each other.

"Fuck," Nedra said.

"This can't be happening," Marilyn whispered.

"No, no, no. This does not make sense. I need to go to Catherine, please."

"I'm sorry, of course," the doctor said. "Let me take you to her room."

"Can we come with her?" Cindy asked.

"Only Dayna can visit her, but you can wait in the CICU waiting room if you like."

"Yes, we'd appreciate that," Stacy said.

In the elevator, the doctor hit the button for the fifth floor. My mind battled to submerge the word *widow-maker* as I built my strength to believe Catherine would be fine. She's strong. She's only sixty.

As we exited the elevator, the doctor pointed toward the waiting area. My friends moved toward it and stood in each other's arms. I turned toward them. Stacy and Marilyn had been Catherine's friends since college. Stacy, her blond hair pulled into a ponytail, was a few inches taller than Marilyn, and Marilyn was a few pounds heavier than Stacy. Cindy, the shortest of the group, and Frieda, her red hair out of control as usual, used her Pentecostal upbringing to pray for all of us. And then there was Nedra, my friend for over thirty years, who sometimes was taken for a man because of her broad shoulders and short spiked blond hair. Their faces struggled to display hope and encouragement. I nodded and walked down the hall.

The doctor and I stepped through the double doors of the CICU and were immediately assaulted by a chorus of beeping monitors. Ten patient rooms with floor-to-ceiling windows ringed the central nursing station. The fluorescent lights illuminated the white tile floors and gleamed off the blue walls designed to give an air of serenity. Electronic monitors flickered from the countertop at the nursing station.

The doctor approached the nurse's desk, flipped through a clipboard full of papers and asked, in a gentle voice, "Ms. Wolford's room, please."

"Room five twenty-four," the nurse responded without looking up.

The doctor nodded thanks and led me down the hallway, our footsteps echoing. My heart pounded in anticipation. When we stopped outside Catherine's door, I felt my palms sweating. I hesitated. My eyes pleaded with the doctor for some sign that she would be lying in bed and greet me with her affectionate smile, telling me she loved me. But his expression remained unreadable.

"She is hooked up to wires and tubes monitoring her heart, blood pressure, oxygen level, and many other things."

I didn't move. I kept searching his eyes.

"You have about ten minutes." He touched my arm and squeezed. "Ten minutes."

My vision blurred as tears pooled in my eyes. I wiped them away with the sleeve of my blouse. I took a deep breath before finally stepping forward, opening the glass sliding door, and entering the threshold.

Beep. Beep. Beep.

I pressed my fingers against my lips and felt tears stinging. Biting down hard, I clenched my jaw.

In the middle of the room, Catherine lay in a hospital bed with raised rails. Her face was gray, and her skin had a bluish tint. A green strap wrapped around both ears kept a mask covering her nose and mouth. Wires were connected to monitors on both sides of her bed, and tubes trailed away from her body into IV bags on metal poles. My throat tightened as I stared at her frail figure.

My fingertips lightly touched her smooth cheek before tenderly caressing her forehead. Leaning over, I placed a gentle kiss on the top of her head.

"Hey, babe, I'm here." I grabbed her hand.

Beep. Beep. Beep.

"I love you, Catherine." I stroked the side of her face with the back of my hand. "Don't give up. You're a fighter." I kissed her cheek. "I need you, Catherine." I laid my forehead against hers.

Beep. Beep. Beep.

I kissed her forehead again and squeezed her hand. "I love you."

My head jerked toward the door as loud voices and footsteps echoed in the hallway. A female voice called, "Stop! Stop! You can't go in."

Vonda Wolford strutted through the door, filling the entire room. Scott followed her, almost as if he were standing in her shadow. Nedra entered last, eyes blazing.

"I'm her mother."

CHAPTER THREE

"Get away from her!"

I stood protectively at Catherine's side, keeping her hand firmly entwined in mine. I inhaled and, in a low and steady voice, said, "You need to back off."

A nurse rushed forward, her hands up in a placating gesture. "Okay, everyone, please take a deep breath and calm down."

"I'm her mother, and this is her brother. *We* are her family." She pointed to me. "Not her!" Vonda said coldly, her body stiff as a board.

She thrust her arm toward me, her manicured fingernail pointing at me. Her eyes blazed with rage as she opened her mouth to speak, and the words came out like ice. "I won't tell you twice. Get out of this room right now."

"Mrs. Wolford, Catherine and I have been partners for fifteen years. I'm staying."

"I don't give a damn," Vonda snapped at me. She turned to Catherine. "You took Catherine away from us with your perverted lifestyle. You brainwashed her into believing she liked women and not men."

Nedra erupted. "Look, you uppity asshole. Dayna was with Catherine when you disowned her and broke her heart."

"Shut up, you butch dyke. My daughter is nothing like you, like any of you."

"Mom, please," Scott said.

"You shut up, too. You went behind my back and had dinner with Catherine"—she pointed to me—"and *her*." Her eyes flashed back to Scott. "I told you. I did not want anything to do with her. I only want Catherine back in the family."

"Mrs. Wolford, I love your daughter, and she loves me."

Beep. Beep. Beep.

Two security guards entered the room with the nurse and doctor.

"Please, all of you must leave now," the doctor said.

"I am not leaving my daughter," Vonda said to her son. "Tell them, Scott. I'm not leaving."

"Mom, please."

"They"—Vonda jabbed a finger at Catherine and then at me—"are not married. That woman has no say over Catherine's care. I'm her *mother*."

I gazed down at Catherine. *Open your eyes. I need to see the eyes that send a lightning bolt to my heart.*

"Get her out of here, and don't let her back in this room. I will make all her medical decisions now." She lifted her chin. "I will take care of her."

I stepped toward Vonda, my eyes ablaze, my face inches from hers. "Just like you've cared for her for the past fifteen years."

Beep. Beep. Beep.

Vonda, her face flushed, retreated. "Get her out of here. Now!"

The security guards moved toward me. I raised my hands. "I'll go." I kissed Catherine before whispering, "I'll be back. I love you."

"Get out! Now!"

My steps quickened and my posture stiffened as I approached Mrs. Wolford.

I met Scott's gaze. Silence stretched between us before I finally mustered the courage to speak. "The last two years mean nothing?" His mouth was half open as if he had been about to reply, but he snapped it shut and hung his head.

Nedra slipped her arm around my shoulder as we entered the hospital hallway. The silence was oppressive, broken only by the soft murmur of the doctor and nurse standing at the end of the corridor. "We're sorry," they said in unison, their words hanging heavily as we walked by.

CHAPTER FOUR

Walking toward the CICU the following day, Nedra said, "Your bloodshot eyes tell me you didn't sleep much last night."

"Every time I close my eyes, I see Catherine lying on the ground or in the hospital bed."

"I am so sorry, Dayna."

"Then I worried about the Wolford powerful connections and what Vonda might do with them. Just last week, Vonda and Bernard's picture was in the Dayton Daily News with Judge Higgins and State Senator Williams at the fundraiser for Dayton Children's Hospital."

"Yeah," responded Nedra, "they have connections throughout the state because of their real estate empire. The Wolford Real Estate Company has huge influence with all sorts of high-up people."

We approached the CICU nurses' station. A nurse stopped us and said, "Sorry, you cannot visit Catherine."

"What do you mean?" I asked.

"The family restricted you and your friends from seeing Catherine."

"What the fuck?" Nedra said.

My jaw clenched, and my hands formed tight fists as I fought to contain my rage. A hot flush crept up my neck and spread across my cheeks. "We've been together fifteen years."

"I don't know what to tell you. You're not legally her family."

I lowered my voice to a whisper. "I *am* her family. She doesn't have anyone but me. I take care of her when she is sick. I am the one who always celebrates her birthday with her. I am the one who consoles her when her mother ignores her phone calls."

"I understand," the nurse said compassionately.

"Do you?" Nedra snapped.

"I am the one who sleeps with her at night and wakes with her in the morning." Tears started to form. "I am the one she loves. I need to see her."

We stood in silence, eyes locked like two opponents in a gunfight, tension rising.

The nurse scanned the hallways. "The family went to eat something. I'll give you five minutes. That's all."

I breathed a sigh of relief and grabbed Nedra's hand.

The nurse grabbed my hand. "She's still in a coma."

The room was illuminated only by the soft glow of medical monitors. Each unit displayed a complicated mixture of waveforms, rhythms, and numbers. Catherine's chest gently rose and fell, but her eyelids were shut amidst the cacophony of beeps.

I kissed her cheek. "Hey, I told you I'd be back." I brushed the hair from her forehead. "Catherine, I don't know when I'll be able to see you again." I leaned my forehead on hers. "Just remember, I love you. And I will fight for us."

The nurse stuck her head around Nedra, standing in the doorway. "The family is coming. You need to go, *now*."

I pressed my lips to Catherine's forehead for a brief moment, then grabbed Nedra's arm and led her toward the stairwell. I opened the door and ushered her out first. Before following suit, I shot one last glance back at the nurse standing vigil by Catherine's room and mouthed my silent gratitude. With a gentle tug, I closed the door behind me.

CHAPTER FIVE

The following afternoon, clouds obscured the sun, and a light, chilly breeze swept over us as our group huddled near the hospital entrance. Cars pulled in and out of the patient loading zone, and a nurse assisted an older woman in a wheelchair into the car's passenger seat.

"Are we ready for this?" Stacy asked.

My voice quivered. "I have got to see her."

"Nedra, where is your lawyer friend?" Marilyn asked.

"Don't worry. She'll be here."

"There she is," Nedra said, and waved.

The woman of medium height marched toward us in her navy-blue power suit, swishing in time with her determined strides. The sun bounced off her glossy black hair, which was pulled back into an intimidating bun, highlighting her strong jawbone and intense blue eyes. "I'm sorry I'm late," she said breathlessly while wiping a few beads of sweat from her forehead. "There was an accident on the interstate, so the usual hour and fifteen-minute drive from Columbus turned into almost two hours."

Nedra touched the woman's arm. "Everyone, this is Leslie McFarlane, the lawyer I told you about who works with me."

I approached her. "Thank you for coming."

She wrapped her arm around my shoulder. "I am so sorry about Catherine. I can't imagine."

"Thanks."

Stacy stepped forward. "So, what is the plan?"

Leslie sighed. "We don't have any legal grounds to stand on, but from my research last night, this is one of the hospitals taking the lead on the new regulations coming out of HHS, which might provide us an opportunity to convince them at least to allow Dayna to visit."

"All we can do is give it our best shot and pray," Frieda said, then bowed her head and said something no one heard.

"Let's do this," Nedra said with a curt nod.

We marched down the corridor. Leslie was at the head of the group, eager to embrace her mission. Her high heels clicked against the floor. Nedra, on one side of Leslie, dressed casually in jeans and a white stretch-cotton shirt and me on the other side. Behind Nedra strode Stacy who wore her everyday teaching outfit of a skirt and a vivid blouse. Frieda followed, clad in her dental hygienist attire, while Marilyn and Cindy trailed behind in their tailored pants, collared dress shirts, and blazers.

Leslie led us through the door to the nurses' station. Three nurses, including the redhead who had let us visit Catherine the previous day, sat and watched various monitors. As one, they stood and glanced at each other and then at us, who must have looked a little like an armed posse.

I read the name tag of the nurse who had helped us. She said, "Ah—please, you need to leave."

"Jessica? Right?"

"Yes."

"Jessica, I am not leaving until I see Catherine." I turned toward her room.

A blond nurse touched my arm. "You are?"

I stopped abruptly. Brittany's name was on her name tag. I stared at her hand on my arm and then at her.

Leslie interrupted, "Hi, I'm Leslie McFarlane. I'm a lawyer from Equality, Ohio. Can we talk for a minute?"

"This is so unfair," a brunette nurse said, her badge showing her name as Kathy.

"I'm really very sorry, but we're only doing our jobs," Brittany said, dropping her hand from my arm. "The family has moved her to a private suite on the eighth floor."

I broke from Marilyn and Cindy's embrace and stood nose-to-nose with Brittany. "What are you talking about?"

Leslie placed her hand on my shoulder. "Dayna, they're not the enemy."

"Look," Jessica said, "we're aware of the ridiculousness of not allowing you to visit your partner. However, we have to follow the family's wishes and the hospital's policies."

"I understand," responded Leslie. "Can you call someone from patient services to meet or direct us to their office?"

"Sure. The office is on the first floor, room one twenty-five."

"Thank you."

Jessica asked, "Dayna, right? I'm—we're"—she turned to Brittany and Kathy, who avoided my gaze—"we're sorry we can't be of more help."

"I understand. Your hands are tied. Thanks again for yesterday."

We reversed course and headed to the first floor.

Huddled in the hospital parking lot, I said, "Thanks, everyone, for coming today. And, Leslie, thanks for your advocacy with patient services, even though they wouldn't budge on going against the family's wishes."

"Dayna, don't give up," Frieda said.

"We'll check in with you tomorrow," Cindy said.

We moved like a synchronized clock in silence, hugging each other and milling about for a minute until we turned to our cars. Cindy clutched Frieda's hand. Marilyn hugged Stacy with one arm.

I slid into the back seat of Leslie's car.

"A lot of good that did," Nedra said from the passenger seat.

"I know. But we had to try," Leslie said from the driver's seat. "I'm sorry I couldn't be more helpful."

I stared out the back window and let the tears fall. My body began to shake, and my teeth chattered. "What am I going to do?"

Nedra jettisoned out of the car, climbed in the back with me, and held my hand. "Your hands are freezing."

"What am I going to do? A heart attack? This is so fucking unfair and so, I don't know, surreal? I love Catherine, and she loves me. Love is love. Why is that so hard for people to understand?"

"Let's get you home."

"No." My finger trembled as I pointed to the imposing hospital. "Catherine is in there. Not at home. How do I fight this? Where is their humanity? Where is their goodness?"

CHAPTER SIX

Wednesday morning, I entered the hospital and sprinted to the information desk. I placed my hands on the counter and leaned in. "Can you please tell me the room for Catherine Wolford?"

The volunteer hit a couple of keys on her computer. She stared at the screen, looked at me and back at the screen, and took a deep breath. "She is not allowed any visitors."

I stepped back from the counter. "What?"

"It says no visitors."

I narrowed my eyes and leaned forward, gazing intently at the volunteer. My voice was low. "Who do I have to talk to about this no-visitor issue?"

"I can call my supervisor?"

"Please do that."

She quickly dialed a number. After a brief conversation, she hung up. "Someone will be here momentarily."

A tall figure clad in a bright-blue ombré blazer came into view. The woman's eyes darted around before meeting my gaze, then her chin rose as if to challenge me. I recognized Ms. Harper as the Director of Patient Services with whom we had spoken the day before.

"Dayna, can we talk in my office?" she asked.

I straightened my back. "No."

The volunteer rolled back her chair and slowly stood, her eyes on us with hawklike intensity.

"Ms. Baldwin," said Ms. Harper. "Please." She tilted her chin to indicate the hallway behind her. "Can we go back to my office?" Her eyes pleaded as they met mine.

"No." I didn't budge. "We can talk right here."

"Okay." She tightened her lips. "Can we at least move to the side so we won't interrupt others who need help?"

We moved closer to the wall.

"Ms. Baldwin, I can imagine how you're feeling right now."

"Really? Have you ever been stopped from seeing the person you love?"

She took a step back. "Ms. Baldwin—"

"I want to see Catherine."

"Ms. Baldwin, the family requested—"

"The family!" The people at the counter turned toward us.

"Please, Ms. Baldwin, keep your voice down."

"I want to see Catherine." I took a deep breath. "Help me be able to see Catherine."

"I cannot allow you to see Ms. Wolford. There are policies."

"You can make exceptions to the policy."

"No, I cannot."

"Anyone can make an exception to a policy. Are you telling me you never have? A person in your position and power as Director of Patient Services?"

"We are not talking about me." She tilted her head to the side. "We are talking about the family requesting that you and your friends not be allowed to visit Catherine."

I shook my head and rubbed my face. "How is that legal? Tell me?"

"You're not family. Mrs. Wolford and Scott are her family. Ms. Baldwin, I'm sorry. Please don't come back to visit Catherine here in hospital. If you do, we will call security and escort you out."

"Really? I'm that much of a threat?"

"That's all I can tell you."

I stared deeply into her eyes. Cutting through the tension, I spat out the words, each syllable enunciating precisely. "And how much, pray tell, did the Wolfords donate to this fine establishment?"

"Ms. Baldwin, it has nothing to do with a donation. It's the law."

"Or lack of compassion. Isn't compassion one of the hospital's core values? Isn't that what I read on one of the wall posters?"

"Yes. It is one of our values."

"So, I guess compassion is only for heterosexuals and people with money." I spun on my heel and strode away, heat rising to my cheeks.

CHAPTER SEVEN

As the sun beat down through the leafy canopy I sat alone in a chair on the back patio of our house, my eyes glazed and unfocused. The neighbor's dog yelping accompanied birds chirping and rustling leaves. My stomach rumbled. I couldn't remember when I had last eaten a full meal or slept for more than a few hours.

I closed my eyes and drifted back to when Catherine and I met. It was a human rights campaign fundraiser in Cincinnati. She was a forty-five-year-old real estate broker in one of the state's top-five real estate development companies and a major contributor to the HRC. I was a thirty-nine-year-old program director at a nonprofit for runaway and homeless youth. We were bidding against each other for dinner for two at St. Elmo's Steak House in Indianapolis, Indiana.

The auctioneer's voice droned, and the room was dimly lit, the only illumination emanating from golden light fixtures high on the walls. I didn't know who was bidding against me until she stood. She was in front of me, off to my right. The spotlight struck her hair like a celestial halo, highlighting her elegant facial features as she turned toward me. The force of her gaze bore into mine, making my heart feel like a lightning bolt had hit it.

She was stunning. Her tall frame, hourglass body, and strawberry-blond, shoulder-length hair framed her high cheekbones and square jaw. She smiled, raised her paddle, and raised the bid.

I smiled and raised my paddle.

We didn't take our eyes off each other as we each bid three times more.

She raised her paddle. The auctioneer said, "Going once, twice." I lowered mine. He slammed the gavel. "Sold." She smiled at me, turned, and disappeared.

I returned to my table, and in front of me were dark-brown eyes and the longest eyelashes I'd ever seen. The scent of her perfume swirled around me.

She stepped forward and held out her hand. Her warm, soft fingers touched mine, and I felt the electricity of her touch as she introduced herself. "Hi. I'm Catherine Wolford."

As the words escaped my lips, my mouth felt dry and my tongue heavy. I could barely whisper them, but I managed to say, "I'm Dayna Baldwin."

"I just won a dinner for two at St. Elmo's," she said, still holding my hand. "Dayna Baldwin, would you like to join me?" Those eyes, that smile, and the upward pull of her lips sent a wave of confidence and seduction crashing over me.

I said yes, and we'd been together ever since. Until now.

"Dayna," Marilyn said as she walked out the patio door, holding a glass of water. She placed the glass on the small circular table between the two chairs.

"Marilyn, how are you?" I asked, my voice cracking. "How's the business? Is there something I can do to help?"

"Don't worry about the real estate business. Our lawyer is reviewing the documents we signed for this situation when we started the Wolford and Jenkins Real Estate Company. I thought Catherine was crazy when she wanted us to take out disability and life insurance on each other."

"Why didn't we see a lawyer?" I closed my eyes and shook my head. "We talked about getting our wills but were focused on getting the new company established after Catherine's parents kicked her out of the family business, remember? We never followed through with wills."

"Dayna."

"Goddamn it." I rocketed out of the chair and took two long strides into the yard. "I haven't seen her in four days." I paced back and forth. "Is she still in a coma, and that's why Vonda is running the show? Otherwise, Catherine wouldn't be letting this happen and she would have contacted me. It hurts, Marilyn, it hurts."

Marilyn guided me back to the chair and handed me the glass of water.

Leslie and Nedra joined us. I stood and faced them. "So, what's next?"

"Equality Ohio will be submitting an injunction to stop the family from prohibiting you visiting Catherine," Leslie said.

"When will they submit the paperwork?"

"Hopefully, this weekend. We're rushing it as fast as we can."

"Thank you, Leslie. I appreciate everything you're doing."

"This is so unfair, and it needs to change. We will do everything we can to help you see Catherine."

"Thanks." I yawned. "I'm going to call the hospital for the umpteenth time to see if I can learn anything. It all seems so futile."

"Don't give up, Dayna," Leslie said as she rubbed my back.

"Yeah, you're the optimist. You always believe everything will work out for the best," Nedra added.

My lips curved into a tight, sad imitation of a smile. My chest had a hollowing ache, gnawing away at any confidence in a positive outcome.

CHAPTER EIGHT

The following day, I was jolted upright by a persistent and demanding thud. The clock's red LED displayed 7:00 a.m. Sighing, I tumbled out of bed, barely avoiding the pile of dirty laundry strewn on the floor. I tossed pants, socks, and T-shirts in the air until I found a pair of jeans and grabbed a hoodie hanging on a chair before heading barefoot to the front door.

I looked out the peephole, and two men who appeared to be NFL linebackers looked back at me. There was a moving truck in the driveway.

I opened the door a few inches. "Yes?"

"Are you Dayna Baldwin?"

I squeezed the door handle. "Who's asking?"

"My name is Mike from Mike's Moving Company, and we're here to pick up some furniture and other belongings from this address."

"I have no idea what you're talking about."

"A Vonda Wolford arranged for us to come."

As I closed the door, my head felt like a spinning top, and my heart pounded. I leaned against the sturdy wood and closed my eyes, desperately trying to understand what Catherine's mother could be doing now.

"Ma'am? Ma'am?"

I rubbed my eyelids until stars sparkled in the fields of my vision. A grimace crossed my face, the kind of smile you make when your mouth tries to be brave, but your heart is filled with fear.

I opened the door and leaned out just enough so Mike saw my face. "Please leave. You are on private property. Please leave now!"

"Ma'am, we have the paperwork right here." He held up the paperwork.

"I don't care. I did not request this, and you are on my property. I am asking you to leave now, or I will call the police."

"Ma'am, please."

"Leave! Now!" I slammed the door in his face.

Both men returned to the truck and backed out of the driveway.

I stumbled through my bedroom, frantically searching for my phone.

"Hey, Dayna. Everything okay?" Marilyn asked.

"No. A moving company was here. Vonda instructed them to come and take furniture and other belongings."

"What did you tell the movers?"

"To get off my property."

"Good. That's a start. I'll call everyone—we'll be over as soon as possible."

"This is getting out of hand, Marilyn. Nothing is making any sense."

"Hang in there, Dayna. I'll be there as soon as I can."

I slowly walked to the living room, my eyes drawn to the bay window at the back of the house. The morning sun rose behind the wooded lot, casting shadows onto the patio. My gaze shifted to the right, the entrance to our bedroom. In my mind's eye, I pictured Catherine walking out of it in her favorite pair of boxers and Tweety Bird T-shirt, coming over to me with those irresistible brown eyes, flashing a mischievous grin, telling me how much she loved me.

My feet thudded against the hardwood floors, sending echoes throughout the living room. My mind raced with endless possibilities of what Vonda might have in store. A familiar engine hum signaled Marilyn's arrival. I bolted for the back door and embraced her as soon as she exited her car. "Thanks for coming, Marilyn."

She hugged me tightly. "This is ridiculous." A man emerged from the passenger side door. "Dayna, this is Mark Huntington, our business lawyer. I thought he could be helpful."

Mark said, "We met briefly when Catherine and Marilyn started their real estate company."

"Yes." I nodded. "I'm sorry. I'm a bit overwhelmed."

"I am so sorry about Catherine. I'll do anything to help."

Marilyn and Mark followed me back toward the house, not saying a word. As I stepped into the house, the rumbling of a truck engine interrupted the silence. We turned and saw a police car following the removalist's truck here earlier.

I raised my hands in the air. "What now?"

We walked through the breezeway from the back to the front of the house and met the police officer.

"Ms. Baldwin?"

"Yes."

"I'm Officer Atkins."

"And?"

"I have papers here signed by a judge, allowing Mrs. Vonda Wolford to retrieve furniture and other belongings of a Catherine Wolford at this address."

"What?"

Mark extended his hand. "I am Ms. Baldwin's lawyer. Let me see those papers, please."

The officer handed them over. I looked at Marilyn and the police officer, who avoided eye contact with me, and then I turned to Mark. "Can she do this?"

He studied the papers and nodded solemnly. "Yes, I'm afraid she can."

"No, no, no." I staggered back. "This is *our* house. This is *our* property. No."

"I'm sorry, Dayna." He touched my arm.

"Well, Catherine isn't dead. She's had a heart attack and is in the hospital."

A car pulled in behind the moving truck.

"Who is that?" I asked. My head spun like a top.

Scott got out of the car and walked toward us.

"What the hell are you doing here?" I asked.

Scott stood before me, unable to meet my gaze. His eyes were rimmed with red, and his usually manicured stubble had grown into a whole, scruffy beard. His tailored suit was rumpled beyond recognition, and his shirt was unbuttoned at the collar without a tie. Tears fell from his eyes when he finally met my gaze. His voice trembled when he spoke, "Dayna," and his lips quivered. "I am so sorry."

My chest heaved, my nostrils flared, and my fists clenched as I yelled, "Sorry about what?"

Marilyn said, "What do you mean you're sorry? Sorry, your mother is taking Catherine's belongings. Sorry you didn't stand up to your mom and support Catherine and Dayna. What are you sorry about?"

"Mom would kill me if she found out I'm here. I just came from the hospital."

"Scott? What are you telling us?" Marilyn asked as she wrapped her arm around me.

Another car pulled into the driveway. Leslie and Nedra jumped out of the car, slammed the doors, and ran toward us with a smile. Leslie waved a sheaf of papers.

My head swiveled between Leslie and Nedra, and Scott and the police officer as the moving van's doors screeched open.

"I'm so sorry," Scott said again.

I stepped until I was face-to-face with Scott. "Sorry about what? Damn it. Just tell me."

Leslie and Nedra skidded to a halt in front of us. Leslie waved the papers. "We got it!" she panted, bouncing from foot to foot. "The judge granted the injunction. You can visit Catherine."

Scott dropped his head. "Catherine died last night."

The papers floated and scattered on the ground.

CHAPTER NINE

After driving four hours to Cleveland and checking into our hotel rooms, Frieda asked, "Are you ready?"

"Ready as I'll ever be, I guess," I answered, turning from gazing out the window.

"I remember how Catherine would love it when we all dressed for a night on the town," Cindy said. "She always liked looking her best when we went out."

I closed my eyes to imagine Catherine in her tight black jeans caressing her firm ass. Her red blouse, showing enough cleavage to entice me to the point of Catherine slapping my hand creeping up her thigh.

"All eyes followed her wherever she walked." Frieda smiled.

Nedra, Marilyn, and Stacy strutted into the room, dressed in their usual ready-for-anything attire of jeans and colorful blouses.

Cindy spun. "We all look fabulous."

"Catherine would approve," I announced.

"Dayna, are you sure you want all of us to go with you?" Stacy asked.

"Absolutely. I want all of you to have time to do what you need." I sighed. "You are our family, and Catherine adored you all." I caught a tear with my finger.

"It's been a week since the funeral," Nedra began, "and that bitch and Scott—"

"Nedra, please. Today is about us saying goodbye to Catherine."

"Well, damn it, Dayna..."

"Nedra." Frieda touched her arm.

"And after everything, they don't let any of us attend the funeral? Who could be so coldhearted?" Nedra cried. "I can't believe she's so evil. It's not fair. She was our friend, our family. She was our Catherine."

Frieda embraced Nedra. I wiped my tears and saw Marilyn and the others doing the same.

Stacy held Marilyn as she said, "I am so sorry, Dayna."

I walked to Marilyn and hugged her. "You were like a sister to Catherine."

"I miss her so much," Marilyn said between sobs. "I expect her to walk through the office door each morning, with Starbucks coffee for all of us."

Marilyn and I hugged, crying in each other's arms.

Stacy rubbed our backs. "Okay, everyone. Let's get going. The drive takes about thirty minutes."

I let go of Marilyn. We stared at each other. "Let's do this. Let's give Catherine the celebration she deserves," she said.

"Who has the champagne?" Nedra asked.

"In the car," Stacy responded.

"Of course, they had to bury her in the family plot," Stacy said as she drove the van with me in the passenger seat.

"Yes, the family's from Cleveland. And, as we guessed, Vonda wanted her family together, even in death," I said, staring out the window as we drove between two tall stone pillars under an iron archway announcing our entrance into Riverside Cemetery.

The driveway curved to the right, then left, as we climbed a slight hill dotted with gravestones of different sizes and shapes. Branches of an old tree reached the sky and covered the driveway. We passed a grave site with newly turned earth and older sites with flowers and American flags. Some stones leaned together like old friends, while others stood tall and straight, asking to be noticed.

As we exited the van, a noisy lawn mower faded into the background, and the smell of fresh-cut grass overwhelmed me.

"I have the map. Her grave..." Stacy swallowed hard. "Her grave should be up a few feet by that lawn crypt and the smaller tree."

I tried to ignore the ache in my heart as we dodged gravestones. The past two weeks had been a blur. I didn't remember the last time I ate a full meal. I hadn't returned to work and was waiting for the probate court proceedings to begin.

"Dayna, we're here," Marilyn said.

My feet halted, and my eyes took in the sight before me: a high, narrow, foolishly ornate coral-green headstone chiseled with Catherine's name, surrounded by freshly cut flowers of various hues. I traced the engravings and felt an icy chill on the stone.

We huddled around the grave in complete silence, each lost in our thoughts and feelings. A breeze blew through the cemetery, shaking the trees and creating a soft rustling. The sun shone brightly on the headstone, reflecting off its surface as if offering some comfort. A single leaf floated down from the tree, twisting and turning in the breeze before resting gently on Catherine's grave.

A loud pop interrupted the silence.

"Champagne, anyone?" Cindy asked.

Stacy and Marilyn poured it into plastic glasses and handed them to everyone.

"To Catherine," Frieda said.

We raised our glasses to the sun. "To Catherine."

After I swallowed, I asked, "Frieda, will you lead us in prayer? Catherine always liked your prayers."

Frieda lowered her head, and we all followed suit.

"Heavenly Creator, we are hurt and angry because we were not allowed to say goodbye to our dear friend Catherine, to be by her side in her time of need."

Marilyn placed her cup on the ground, grabbed my hand, and started a chain of everyone holding hands until we enclosed Catherine's headstone in a circle of friendship and love.

"Give us the strength to forgive, heal, laugh, and continue to love as Catherine would want us to. Provide Dayna the courage to deal with losing her best friend, lover, and life partner. Provide hope for all of us that the goodness in people will prevail.

"Join us now as we remember and celebrate the life of Catherine Wolford. A woman who lived life to its fullest. A woman who loved and supported other women. Catherine gave back to the community in many ways to ensure others had the opportunities her privilege had provided her. A woman whose laughter was contagious. May we always be reminded to tell and show others they are loved, as Catherine always told us. Peace be with you all."

"Thank you, Frieda."

"Remember when Catherine described how to get into a kayak, and she made it sound so sexual?" Cindy said.

"Oh, that was funny," Marilyn laughed.

"What about the time..." Stacy began.

We stood in a solemn circle around the headstone. Memories of Catherine's life filled the air with stories of her contagious laughter, her passion for helping others, and that one time she was arrested while protesting for abortion rights. As we shared our reminiscences, salty tears ran down my cheeks, united with the taste of champagne on my lips. I felt humbled to be celebrating the life of this remarkable woman with those who had known her best and yet were all so broken by the finality of her death. Every ounce of emotion around me seemed to reflect our immense love for Catherine.

"Dayna, we'll give you some time alone," Frieda said as she touched my shoulder, and Cindy kissed my cheek.

Marilyn and Stacy stood at the gravestone's side. "We love you and miss you, Catherine." Marilyn kissed her fingers and placed them on the headstone. They turned and walked away.

"This is so unfair. I'm not sure I'll ever get over this anger toward the Wolford family," Nedra said, tears flowing down her face. "I'm not gonna stop fighting for LGBTQ and marriage equality, Catherine." She sniffled. "Never."

Nedra touched my shoulder and left.

Alone with Catherine, I fell to my knees.

"Catherine, honey, I miss you so much. What am I going to do without you?" I brushed the petals of a flower. "We were going to grow old together, remember?" I smiled. "We all joked about our younger friends pushing us in our wheelchairs and feeding us smoothies with straws. Remember?" I raised my face to the sky. "Catherine, I don't believe I can ever forgive your mother and family for what they did to us, to me."

As the breeze picked up, I placed one hand on the cold, green grass, and the other traced Catherine's name. A shiver ran from my shoulder down the length of my arm.

"I will always be thankful you outbid me on the dinner." I took a deep breath. "Because I don't know if I would've dared to ask you. You were so attractive and confident and, if I must say, sexy." I smiled. "I thought I would never have a chance with you." I kissed my fingers and placed them on her name. "Catherine, you are my first love, and I will always love you. Rest in peace, my love, rest in peace."

Suddenly, a dove landed on Catherine's headstone and released a high-pitched coo. It was stunning. The dove retook flight and perched on a nearby tree like a sentry guarding its kingdom. I saw Catherine's smile in my mind's eye, and suddenly, overwhelmingly, I felt lighter.

CHAPTER TEN

June 26, 2015

"I can't wait until Leslie gets here," Nedra said as we gathered in Marilyn and Stacy's living room. Her excitement was palpable, filling the room with warmth and excitement.

We had spent many nights here, huddled by the fireplace, having heated political discussions and much lighthearted laughter. We had supported each other with understanding and encouragement through our individual journeys. Those late nights in this cozy home had created an unbreakable bond between us.

"This is such a historic day. Who would have believed it?" Marilyn said as she embraced Stacy.

"Well, I didn't believe it, and it was hard to control my excitement. I was in the teachers' lounge and saw on the TV that the Supreme Court had finally legalized same-sex marriage," Stacy said.

I stood in the living room doorway, taking in the scene. My friends jumped and shouted joyfully, embracing each other with a newfound sense of validation. Smiles stretched across their faces as they discussed this monumental decision.

With her arm around Stacy, Marilyn asked, "How did the other teachers react?"

"Most of them cheered. One or two grunted and said something about the world ending." We all laughed.

"It's always the homosexuals' fault," Nedra said.

Cindy and Frieda dashed past the large window to the right and crashed through the front door. Frieda huffed and puffed. "Can you believe it? My Pentecostal parents are rolling in their graves."

Cindy wrapped Marilyn and Stacy in a bear hug. "I can't believe it. It finally happened." Frieda hugged Nedra.

It *was* a historic day for the LGBTQ community. If only it had happened six years ago. Catherine and I would've been married, and I would've been by her side, holding her, when she died.

Instead, because Catherine did not have a will, Mark Huntington battled with Wolford's lawyers for three years to complete the probate process. The result was Vonda repossessing Catherine's belongings and me keeping the house since we had joint ownership on the mortgage.

But each morning I'd wake up, and she wouldn't be next to me, telling me how much she loved me or how lucky we were to have each other. I couldn't tickle her when I greeted her as she walked in from work and told her she was the love of my life. The house was sad. I was sad.

One night, it all came to a head after being with my friends for dinner. They'd given me a hard time about the crumbs all over my place setting and me, just as Catherine always had.

I'd shuffled into our bedroom, shouldering the door closed behind me. I slid down its length, pressing my back against the cold wood, and felt very alone. Everything in the room reminded me of her and her absence. No soft touch of her fingers against my skin, no gentle caresses that sent shivers through my body, no passionate entwining in delirious lovemaking.

Tears spilled down my cheeks, releasing the pain I'd buried for years—anger, hurt, sadness, emptiness, guilt, and regret. Everything tumbled out in grief-stricken sobbing.

I sold our house, bought land, and built a thirteen hundred-square-foot, three-bedroom cabin in the country outside Trotwood, a suburb of Dayton, and down the road from Marilyn and Stacy. I stepped down from my role as executive director at Sunrise House, a nonprofit devoted to helping homeless teenagers find shelter, housing, and employment. My journey with the organization began as a humble counselor, but over the years, I gained valuable skills and experience that led me to launch my consultancy, Baldwin Executive Coaching for Women. In addition, I sponsored the Catherine Wolford Charity Golf Outing to support the American Heart Association's education program for women.

Around that time, Marilyn informed me that the realtor she had hired, Rebecca Copeland, whom she'd hired six months after Catherine died, would become her new partner in the company. Someone younger who could carry on the business when she retired. This was another sign it was time for me to move on.

When I realized I was compartmentalizing my life, and feelings of unworthiness were creeping back into my psyche, I returned to therapy for about a year.

And now, two years later, I was celebrating marriage equality with my friends.

"I bet Leslie is ecstatic," Cindy said as she hugged Nedra.

Nedra said, "All I can tell you is that I cried when I heard it and hugged everyone in our office. Dayna, what do you think?"

"I think it's about time."

"Nedra, you and Leslie gonna tie the knot?" Marilyn asked.

"Well, it's been six years." Nedra looked at me. "Sorry, Dayna."

"Don't be sorry. I'm happy for you."

"But we never would've gotten to know each other if we hadn't worked on yours and Catherine's situation."

"Nedra. It's okay."

My gaze swept around the room, and I couldn't help but feel a pang of loneliness. I wondered if anyone again would be there to welcome me home with a hug and a kiss.

"Dayna?" Marilyn said. "You okay?"

"Yeah, I'm fine. I'm just thinking about what I must pack for next week's trip."

"Where are you going this time?" Cindy asked.

"D.C. for the National Conference for Women in Business."

"Do you need a ride to the airport?"

"No, thanks. I'll leave my car." There was a knock at the door. "I got it." They continued to discuss today's event.

When I opened the door, Leslie leaped in to embrace me. "We won!" she said, then released me. "Where is my woman?"

I tilted my head toward the living room.

She glided across the room, her hands in impeccably tailored pants pockets. Slowly, she knelt before Nedra, her neck craned to look up into her eyes.

Everyone stopped talking and turned. Nedra's mouth dropped open. "Leslie, what are you doing?"

"Nedra." Leslie pulled out a small black box and opened it. "Will you marry me?"

Nedra's hands covered her mouth, and her eyes filled with tears. Her mouth was moving, but nothing came out.

"I've never seen Nedra speechless," Frieda said.

"Nedra?" Stacy bounced up and down. "What's your answer?"

Nedra cried and reached for Leslie's hands. Leslie slowly pulled her up. "Yes! Yes!"

Leslie's hands trembled as she slowly pulled the ring out of the box. With a gentle smile, she placed it on Nedra's finger and watched as her eyes lit up. Nedra grabbed Leslie's face and kissed her passionately. The tears that streamed down Nedra's cheeks were a reminder of the pure love they shared.

They finally broke their kiss. Nedra ran her hands through Leslie's long black hair. "I love you," she said.

"I love you too," Leslie said, wiping away Nedra's tears.

"Our first proposal!" Stacy cheered.

Their joy shone like the sun breaking through the clouds.

I walked out of the house, grabbed a beer from the patio refrigerator, and sat by the pool. I raised the beer bottle to the sky. "To marriage equality." And guzzled it.

CHAPTER ELEVEN

"As I mention in my book, when you align your values with your leadership style and be authentically who you are, there is congruence and consistency in your life and the lives of the people working with you."

A younger woman with blond hair, who looked like she could recognize expensive vintage wine, sat in the middle row of tables. Every time our eyes met, she smiled and tilted her head as if curious about what I would say next. She lowered her eyes, reached for the necklace on her chest near her cleavage, and twirled the chain in her finger.

"Ms. Baldwin?"

The moderator repeated, "Ms. Baldwin, any last words for the group?"

"Oh, yes. True leadership is predicated on what we do." My eyes met the blonde, who was now licking her lips. "What we do has the most impact and meaning."

"Ms. Baldwin's book, *Women as Leaders*, highlights her five-step formula to clarifying your values, beliefs, and purpose to be authentic and intentional with your communication and actions so you can confidently and powerfully inspire others to follow you as a leader. It is available for purchase."

"I'm happy to sign anyone's book."

"Thank you, Ms. Baldwin," the moderator said.

"Thank you for having me and for all of you attending. Since this is the last session of the day, enjoy your evening."

Applause erupted.

Women bombarded me with questions. Some wanted more information about my coaching business, so I handed each of them my business card and told them to call me to discuss the details.

After twenty minutes of mingling, I weaved between tables and collected leftover handouts. Then I heard, "Ms. Baldwin?"

I slowly turned and took in the woman from the middle table. Her bold eyes were a deep, velvety brown, her nose was slightly upturned, and her full lips were curved into a gentle smile. A bronze hue spread across her cheeks and down her long neck. She stepped closer. "Can I talk with you about your coaching and the cost of your services?"

I continued to collect the handouts. "What's your name?"

"My name is Victoria. Victoria Abernathy. I'm the vice president of a bank."

"Hello, Victoria. Nice to meet you."

"And I want to become the president of the bank."

I stuffed the handouts into my briefcase. "Oh, I see."

"I believe you can teach me how to explode through the glass ceiling." Her red lips formed an exaggerated *o* when she said the word explode.

"Explode. Interesting word choice." I gazed around at the empty tables and chairs. We were the only ones there, and all the doors were closed.

"I've dedicated my career to reaching that ultimate goal. I have this drive deep within me, this fire, and I can't stop the burning." She walked toward me until the back of my thighs bumped into a table.

I placed my hands on her slim waist and drew her to me. "I can help increase the heat to keep the fire burning and devise a plan for you to explode through the glass ceiling."

She rested her hands on my shoulders. "I would like that very much."

I leaned closer, our cheeks touched, and whispered, "Why don't we go somewhere more private to discuss how to keep the fire burning?"

"How about my room?" Victoria asked.

"Works for me."

"Say in about forty-five minutes, room six twenty-three?"

"I'll bring the wine."

"I'll be waiting." She kissed my cheek and walked away.

I watched her walk, admiring the toned calves and the curves of her ass, exquisitely framed by her fitted skirt.

I stood outside room six twenty-three with a bottle of the most expensive wine I could purchase from the hotel bar. I knocked.

"Please come in."

The door opened slowly. I entered the room and walked past Victoria, who stood before the closed door and facing me. She wore a red silk robe that stopped midthigh. The sleeves draped across her arms, unmasking a shoulder and a swatch of skin across her chest. The robe was tied loosely at the waist, showing off her flat stomach and voluptuous breasts.

I walked toward her. My libido started to rev up at the sight of her untying her robe. I lifted the bottle. "I brought the wine. But I need you to understand I'm not looking for a relationship, and what happens tonight stays between us."

The robe fell to the floor. "Whatever you say, Ms. Baldwin."

I dropped the bottle of wine onto the bed. Her breasts were full, and her prominent nipples were teasing to be pinched and licked.

She stepped toward me and started to unbutton my blouse, one by one, as I continued to admire her firm stomach and legs.

"You didn't wear a bra," she said, lowering my blouse off my shoulders, exposing my nipples that stood at attention. "And you're excited." She brushed her hand over my breasts, causing me to release a loud moan.

I ran my hand through her hair as she unzipped my jeans, lightly touching my stomach with the back of her hand. "Why me?" I asked.

"Why not you?"

"I'm much older than you, and my body isn't what it used to be."

"I've always been attracted to older women. Older women are wiser and more experienced in life. And as you say, you can show me how to keep the fire burning. I'm a quick learner." She pushed down my pants and underwear in one motion.

"Seems like you're experienced in some other things as well."

She kissed my stomach above my pubic hair and continued upward, kissing each of my breasts until we stood face-to-face, competing to see who was breathing harder.

"Before I make you explode." I reached and massaged both of her breasts. "We agree that what happens tonight stays between us?" I continued to fondle her breasts and licked her neck.

Victoria gasped and licked her lips. "Yes."

"Yes, what?"

"I agree."

"And?"

"And yes, please show me." I grabbed her waist and pulled her close, and as she leaned her forehead on mine, her eyes turned dark with lust. "Make me explode."

Our lips crashed together. Our hands tangled in each other's hair as we both groaned. I placed my leg between hers, and she stepped closer. Her excitement was intoxicating as she rubbed against my leg.

"For an older woman, you're strong," she whispered in my ear between moans.

"As you say, wiser and more experienced. Now, I want you on the bed, on your back." I bit her ear.

She slid off my leg and lay on the bed, her blond hair splayed over the pillow.

"Spread your legs. Hands over your head. Keep them there."
I walked to the end of the bed.

Victoria placed her hands over her head and entwined her fingers.

I climbed onto the bed and slowly lowered myself onto her. My hips arrived between her legs while I kissed her neck. Her hips jumped to meet mine as my lips descended toward the target.

"Please," Victoria said, goose bumps spreading over her body.

"Patience."

I kissed, bit, and licked until I reached her thigh's apex and center of pleasure.

"Oh, God," she said as she lifted her hips off the bed and reached for my head.

"Arms over your head. No touching me. I do the touching."

She raised her arms as I dove into her heat with my mouth wide open.

"Oh, Ms. Baldwin." Victoria's hands grabbed the sheet, and her hips moved against my mouth.

Her sounds were animalistic, and she asked between breaths, "Please, Ms. Baldwin, can I come?"

She tried to control her orgasm. Her breathing became erratic. The whole bed shook.

She begged, "Please!"

I removed my mouth. "Explode for me, now."

I returned, and her body arched as she screamed.

I removed my mouth and kissed her labia goodbye. I gently kissed her stomach and followed a path of butterfly kisses up to her chest. My mouth stopped at the tip of her neck and softly pressed against it before I trailed, and whispered in her ear, "Were there fireworks with your explosion?"

"Most definitely." She caressed my face.

"Mission accomplished."

"Okay, give me a few minutes to recover, and I'll show you what I can do for you."

I kissed her forehead and climbed off her.

"Wait, where are you going?"

"I'm going back to my room."

"But."

"My rules."

She leaned on her elbows, and her confusion was evident. "But I want to touch you."

"Not necessary. The pleasure is all mine."

"Hold on." She sat up and covered herself with the sheet.

"Look, Victoria," I said as I found my clothes and put them on, "I prefer to please others."

"What about you?"

"I take care of myself."

"Dayna, please stay."

"Not happening. Good night, Victoria." I opened the door and walked out.

CHAPTER TWELVE

I was on my last Zoom call when, from the corner of my eye, I saw Marilyn standing in the doorway, waving her arm. She gestured toward the living room. I raised one finger, assuring her I'd be done soon, and continued my call.

"Jennifer, I'm so glad you followed up with me after the Lancaster conference. Talk to you soon. Have a productive week." I hung up. I leaned back in my chair and stretched my arms over my head, then gathered my pages of notes and stuffed them into a folder.

"Marilyn, come on in."

"Wow!" Marilyn flopped into the leather chair across my desk with a thud. "Your desk looks like a tornado went through it. Rough day?"

"Sorry." I gathered more papers and stacked them on top of more papers. "A client needed to discuss an emergency concerning an employee situation. It threw off my schedule."

"How was D.C.?"

"Same old, same old. A few women have contacted me for my coaching services." My cell phone rang. "Excuse me. It might be the client from this morning."

"No. Go ahead."

"Hello, Baldwin Executive Coaching for Women." I turned away from Marilyn as heat radiated up my neck. After a few seconds, I hung up and turned to face Marilyn.

"One of your one-night stands from your last conference?" Marilyn asked, staring at me.

I stared back at her. "Maybe."

"You do not need to be hooking up with strangers."

"Do you realize how hard it is to meet lesbians my age? They're either in relationships or not interested in a relationship."

"Don't you think it's time to move on?"

"I have." I pointed to the walls. "I built a new house and started my own business."

"You know I'm not discussing that part of your life." She imitated my pointing to the walls. "Please talk to me about how you're feeling."

"That's what my therapist would have asked me." I laughed.

"So"—Marilyn raised an eyebrow—"you didn't learn anything in your therapy sessions a few years back?"

"Yeah. I learned how I protect myself from rejection." I was becoming defensive. "And it's up to me to determine when I'm ready to implement new strategies in my life."

"Oh, good one, Miss Executive Coach." Marilyn rolled her eyes.

"Marilyn," I sighed, then smiled. "We have been friends for over twenty years. I cherish our friendship and appreciate your concern, but, I'm okay. My business is going well. I'm doing another workshop next month, so I should increase my client list. I'm contemplating hiring a part-time administrative assistant."

Marilyn's eyes scanned my desk. "Well, from the look of your desk, that might be good. But I'm not talking about your business life. I'm talking about your personal life."

"You mean my love life?"

"Yes. You're a wonderful woman with a lot to offer. If only you would let someone in."

I walked to the window and crossed my arms over my chest. "I'm not sure I want to."

"You can't allow what Vonda did to impact the rest of your life." Marilyn walked to my side and put her arm around my shoulder.

"I'm not sure I can love anyone again." I leaned on Marilyn's shoulder.

She pulled me close. "Give yourself a chance. Don't you think Catherine would want you to be happy?"

"Probably, I guess. So, what about you and Stacy? Have you picked a date for your wedding?"

"No, and stop changing the subject. At least come with us this Saturday to the Neon. We're going to the matinee and then to the Trolley Stop in the Oregon District for an early dinner and drinks."

I escaped her embrace, collected more papers on my desk, and put them in a file folder. "What movie?"

Marilyn explained that the movie was about Alan Turing and how he decrypted German intelligence messages during World War II before being chemically castrated.

I sighed. "Sounds lovely. What time?"

"We're meeting at the Neon at twelve thirty, and the movie starts at one."

"Okay, just to get you off my back."

Marilyn hugged me. "I'm glad. Everyone will be happy to see you." As we walked into the living room, she asked, "So I overheard your client say you've worked out a payment plan with her. I thought you had a sliding scale?"

"I do. She's the CEO of a small adoption agency in Pennsylvania, and I gave her an additional discount."

"So, it's okay to be kind to others, but you don't trust others will be kind back?"

"Something like that."

CHAPTER THIRTEEN

With wet hair and in just underwear, I stood in my walk-in closet. I scanned blouses, dress slacks, and casual wear hanging on rods on either side, organized by color. Folded tees and sweaters were in the cubbies. My closet was organized, like my life. Work went on the closet rods. Socialization was stacked in the cubbies. My sex life was my shoes scattered all over the floor. And my feelings? I turned in a circle. It seemed I didn't have room for them.

I moved the hangers until I found my black jeans and a gray, three-quarter-sleeve, lightweight V-neck top that hung and covered my belly. I slipped on my black Vans with the white stripe down the side, finished dressing, and headed out the door.

My friends stood off to the left in the Neon's small lobby, crowded with round tables and chairs. Posters plastered on the walls announced upcoming movies. Off to the right, people milled about in front of the concession stand, waiting to order locally brewed beer, wine, fresh popcorn, or espressos. I bought my ticket and a beer.

Surrounded by the group, I sipped on the cold beer as we discussed our luck of living in the quiet suburbs of Dayton, ideally situated between the bustling cities of Cincinnati and Cleveland and Columbus and Indianapolis.

"Anyone want anything from the bar?" Frieda asked. She distributed our drinks and popcorn as we moved toward the two small theaters, going to the one on the right.

Leslie held up her popcorn bag at the far end of the row. "Popcorn, anyone?"

"Sure," Cindy said.

"Open up." Leslie threw a piece of popcorn in the air. Cindy caught it in her mouth. We hooted and hollered.

Leslie threw another piece at me, and I caught it, chewed, and swallowed. "Tastes pretty good."

"Yeah, that's my Dayna," Nedra said.

Frieda said, "Come on. You're acting like teenagers."

We shrugged, and I said, "What's wrong with that?"

"Yeah, Frieda," Nedra chortled, "what's wrong with that?"

"Okay, throw one to me," Frieda said.

We all cheered in unison, "Frieda. Frieda. Frieda."

Leslie threw a handful of popcorn, and Frieda moved her head and caught one piece while the rest fell around her. We clapped.

"You're good with your mouth," Leslie said.

Cindy turned, wiggled her eyebrows at Frieda, and opened her mouth to say something.

Frieda pointed her finger at her. "Don't you even go there."

Cindy covered her mouth and laughed under her breath. The lights dimmed.

Stacy said, "You're worse than my students."

Near the movie's end, Turing was convicted of gross indecency and chose chemical castration. My tears started to fall.

"Oh, God, no," Frieda said, and Cindy grabbed her hand.

The credits rolled, and the theater's lights slowly turned on. We all sat silently for a few minutes.

"Well, that was uplifting," Nedra said.

"I need a drink," added Marilyn.

"It was back in 1938," Stacy said.

Frieda's voice quivered with disbelief and disgust. "How can a society stoop so low? It's inhumane!"

I rose from my seat. The anger bubbled inside me, threatening to spill over. "Ask Vonda." I spat out her name like venom. "She would know all about it." My fists clenched, my shoulders feeling the weight of injustice.

CHAPTER FOURTEEN

Marilyn and Stacy walked to the beat of their conversation as they strode ahead of us, with Nedra and Leslie trailing behind. Cindy and Frieda kept step with me, our feet clapping against the pavement. The brick road of the historic Oregon District of Dayton was dotted with waxy-leaved trees that stood sentinel, while signs above boasted galleries, unique shops, pubs, and coffee houses. People strolled along the sidewalk, stopping to admire storefronts or chat with friends, while others walked their dogs or lingered outside cafes.

We passed a sex shop. "I always wanted to go into this store," Nedra said.

Leslie stopped. "Why?"

"Curiosity."

"Oh?" Leslie grabbed Nedra's arm and kissed her cheek. "Tell me more."

The others sauntered on to the bar ahead, but I paused to peer into the sex-shop window. My eyes darted from a feather boa to blindfolds of velvet and leather to handcuffs with fur lining.

My mind went back to a month before Catherine's death. We had just returned from a date night and were undressing each other, clothes flying everywhere, leaving a trail from the front door to the bedroom. We stood naked, facing each other in front of the bed, my heart pounding and Catherine breathless. Catherine had ordered me to lie on my back on our king-sized bed. I'd jumped, turned in the air, and laughed as I landed in the middle of the bed. Catherine had shaken her head. "I love your laugh."

Then, without warning, she pounced with a growl, her knees landing between my legs. "Now I'm going to eat you. But first." She reached for the side table, opened the drawer, and pulled out a red scarf. She placed it over my eyes, leaned forward so her breasts touched my face, and tied it behind my head. "Now we're ready." She touched my shoulders and slowly pushed me back onto the bed.

"Please," I'd begged.

Catherine leaned in and whispered, "Remember we talked about keeping your hands to yourself while I fuck you?"

"Catherine." I raised my hips.

"You told me you want me to talk dirty to you, right?"

I nodded frantically.

"So, you ready to be eaten?"

I nodded again.

"I can't hear you."

Between breaths, I said, "Yes."

"Are you sure?"

"Yes. Please." My body trembled in anticipation of what was to come.

A hand on my shoulder brought me back to reality. "Dayna? Did you hear my question?" Cindy asked.

"Uh, no." I turned from the window. "Sorry. What was the question?"

With a furrowed brow, Cindy asked, "Dayna? I asked if you saw something of interest?"

I shook my head. "Like Nedra said, just curious."

Marilyn shouted, "Come on, I can't hold this door forever."

The door creaked as we entered the Trolley Stop, and the scent of aged wood filled our noses. The walls were paneled with dark-stained oak, and the grain danced in and out of sight as light glimmered through uneven gaps. We walked along the bar, tracing our fingers over its smooth, glossy surface until we reached a few people chatting and clinking glasses. A host with kind eyes guided us up two steps to the right, where a massive wooden table sat surrounded by eight hardwood chairs that groaned in welcome as we took our seats.

We searched the menus and placed our food and drink orders. We discussed the movie, and our conversation led to Cindy sharing she was a KAP.

"What's that?" Marilyn asked.

"It's a Kink Aware Professional."

"Cool," Nedra said.

"Kink?" Marilyn asked.

"Yeah. Like BDSM, consensual nonmonogamy, and fetishes. You know, those types of things."

"Okay, I'm gonna ask," Nedra started. "Any of you into kink?"

Leslie bumped her shoulder into Nedra. "That's a personal question."

Nedra's eyes scanned the group. "We're all friends."

"I strongly believe if people talked about sex, sexuality, intimacy, and what gives them pleasure, we'd all be more satisfied in bed," Cindy said.

We all turned to her, and our eyes widened.

"Is that the voice of experience or the social-work professional talking?" Marilyn asked.

Cindy lifted her shoulders, turned to Frieda, and smiled.

"Frieda! No way," Nedra said. "The girl who grew up in the church and went to Bible school every summer until she was eighteen?"

Frieda's face turned beet red. "So, because I live with and love a KAP, you assume we're a kinky couple?"

"Are you?" I asked.

No one said a word as all heads turned toward Cindy and Frieda.

Frieda sat straight and put her arm around Cindy. "Yes, Cindy is my submissive."

Everyone gasped.

"No way," Stacy and Leslie said at the same time.

Frieda laughed. "Got ya."

Everyone exhaled, and Nedra's elbows fell heavily onto the table. "Bummer."

"Boy," Frieda said, holding out her hand. "I had you all in the palm of my hand. Cindy is not my submissive, but we talked about her work as a KAP, and I'm learning a lot." Frieda moved a strand of hair behind Cindy's ear. "Who knows where it will lead?"

As we continued with dinner, Marilyn asked, "Dayna, how do you do it?"

"What?"

"The crumbs." She pointed to the bread crumbs surrounding my plate.

"Catherine never understood how crumbs were all over you and on the table," Stacy said.

I smiled, remembering the date a few weeks before Catherine died. We'd visited Boca's in Cincinnati, a fancy restaurant with soft lighting, tasteful artwork, white linen tablecloths, and napkins.

At the end of the dinner, Catherine smiled and shook her head. "Dayna." She pointed to my plate. She reached for my hand. "I enjoy watching you. You savor every bite."

My eyes bore into hers. "Yes. Every bite."

I'd woken in Catherine's arms the following day, bite marks on my shoulder and breast.

"Dayna, are you listening?" Stacy asked.

"Yes. She loved that I savored every bite." I smiled.

The server brought our bills and interrupted my racing thoughts of Catherine, me, and our last couple of months of lovemaking.

We walked back toward our cars parked across the street from the Neon, passing patios filled with patrons for dinner and eclectic music flowing from various coffee shops, bars, and breweries.

Leslie hung back with me. "You seem a bit distracted tonight. How are you doing?"

I shrugged. "I'm hanging in there."

"Have you thought about dating?"

We split and went around a family of four walking toward us. The young children were holding ice cream cones and almost ran into us. A woman carrying a little girl with pigtails smiled apologetically. A boy with a dripping cone wore a look of concentration on his face.

"Sorry, am I overstepping with my dating question?"

"No, but I'm not sure if I want to be looking at someone my age."

"How old are you?"

"Sixty."

"Oh, come on. That's not old in 2015."

I chuckled. "I keep myself busy with my coaching business. Besides, what else do I need right now?"

"Well, I believe you have many more years to share your sense of adventure and humor with someone"—she waved her hand in a circle—"waiting for you out there in the universe."

We both chuckled.

"Thanks, Leslie, but I'm fine." We passed the metal gateway on the other side of the street and left the Oregon District. I hung my head, then raised it as I hooked my arm in Leslie's. "I'm fine."

CHAPTER FIFTEEN

The golf-outing committee asked me to pick up the paper products, so Saturday morning, I was in my sweaty golf blouse, shorts, and Croc flip-flops. No matter how early the tee time in July, it was always hot and humid when you reached the eighteenth green.

My squeaky cart wheeled over the cold tile floor as I strayed from aisle to aisle of the massive grocery store. Oldies music filled my ear, and fresh produce's pungent odors made me smile. As I rounded the corner, I sidestepped an unattended cart parked in the middle of the aisle and an elderly couple reaching for granola bars on a top shelf. I offered to get it for them. They smiled and said thank you.

My phone rang.

"Hey, Susan, the best golf outing organizer in the world, what's up?"

"Where are you?"

"I'm in Meijer, shopping for the American Heart Association golf outing."

"Okay, so—"

I turned right. "Susan, what's the problem?"

"I received a team registration form from Scott Wolford."

"What?" I came to a complete halt.

"Yeah. Scott Wolford."

I leaned on the cart's handlebar and ran my fingers through my sweaty hair.

"You there, Dayna?"

"Yeah. He's always donated, but he's never registered a team."

"I know. Scott's previous donations," Susan continued, "were personal, not from the business. But this team is registered under Wolford Real Estate Company."

"What?" Again, I jerked to a stop.

"Yeah. And the company is also sponsoring a couple of holes."

"In the name of the Wolford company?" I rubbed my eyes. "I wouldn't believe Vonda would allow him to donate."

"Well, he has a team, and they've sent in their registration and entrance fee."

I rounded the corner, eyes searching the shelves, when off to the right, a cart suddenly appeared. I swerved my cart, the ends of the handlebars of both carts crashing together and my shin hitting the bottom ledge of the other cart. Wincing, I muttered an obscenity under my breath as I stumbled back.

"Are you okay?"

"Yes, I ran into a cart." I rubbed my shin. "He paid. He plays."

"Okay. I thought you should know."

"Thanks for the warning."

I continued to rub my shin and locked eyes with a stunning woman. Her light, golden-brown hair contrasted her dark-gray chino shorts and bright-pink, short-sleeved V-neck.

She raised one finger and said, "Sorry," turning to an older woman taking cans off the shelf.

I pushed my cart around them. "Next time, keep the cart with you, will you? You're blocking the aisle."

She turned to me. Her hazel eyes pleaded for understanding, which made me hesitate as she apologized again. "Sorry."

The older woman turned and asked the younger woman, "Does she teach with you?"

"No, Mom."

As I walked away, I overheard her. "Come on, Mom. We have enough soup cans in our cart."

I was at the self-service checkout machine closest to the exit when I saw the woman and her mom walking toward the door. The mom pushed the cart, and the younger woman's hand was on the handlebar, helping guide the cart. "So, you want hamburgers on the grill tonight?"

The woman's muscular, tanned legs strode with confidence. She spotted me staring. When she recognized me, I dipped my head, acknowledging her.

"Hamburgers? Yes, I do. Did we buy chips?"

"Yes, Mom, Mikesell's. Your favorite."

She looked over her shoulder, and they disappeared through the exit.

CHAPTER SIXTEEN

The sky was a crisp, powdery blue, and swaths of cumulus clouds spiraled over my car as I drove to Beechwood Golf Course for our charity outing. The cool breeze through my open windows helped me forget about the piles of folders on my desk and reminded me to focus on having fun today.

The parking lot was half empty and the early-morning tee time golfers had finished. Some were sitting in their golf carts, adding up their scores while others threw their clubs into their trunks.

I found a space facing the practice putting green, where Frieda stood over her ball, turned her head toward the hole, and back over the ball. She stroked the ball. It rolled past the hole and off the green.

I jumped out and yelled, "Hey, crusher. You need to control all that power."

"Hey, Dayna." She walked down the slight slope into the rough and picked up her ball.

"Frieda, thank you for soliciting donations for the outing. You're amazing."

"Oh, it's just like trying to recruit people to follow the Lord. You keep pushing the benefits of joining and how it'll make your life better and more fulfilled."

"Frieda. Frieda. Frieda." I smiled.

"Now," she demanded, "help me with my putting."

I told her it's all about the pace. She walked back to the green and muttered, "Pace. Pace. Pace."

I leaned my elbows on the top rung of the fence railing as she lined up her putt.

She stroked the ball confidently this time and it rolled right into the cup. Frieda pumped her hand in the air. "Look out, Lexi Thompson, here I come."

As I walked into the pro shop, past the kitchen area, and entered the meeting room, sunlight from the floor-to-ceiling windows brightened the room. Susan directed volunteers to set up the registration table and organize the silent auction and prize tables. Volunteers were also in the kitchen, organizing pots and pans for the food after everyone completed their round of golf.

I turned to the volunteers. "Good morning, everyone. Everything is looking great. Thank you for all your efforts and time. I appreciate you all."

The volunteers waved. "You're welcome."

"No problem."

"Glad to help."

My lips curled into a gentle smile, and a warmth spread through my chest. Catherine would be proud to see how our efforts, in her name, continued to impact women.

"Hey, Dayna," Marilyn said as she walked in with Rebecca.

"Hi, Rebecca. Good to see you again." I hugged her. "Marilyn tells me you've been practicing your drive?"

"Yeah, I took lessons at the end of last season. So, beware"— she pointed toward herself—"this youngster is ready for the battle for the longest drive."

I met and greeted golfers as they headed to the registration table to check in, thanking them for coming and making a special effort to greet hole sponsors and other significant contributors. Then I headed back to the practice putting green.

My team of Marilyn, Stacy, Rebecca, and our competitors, Nedra, Cindy, and Frieda, practiced chipping and putting as golfers loaded their clubs into carts.

"Hey, Nedra. Where's Leslie?" I asked. "We start in about forty-five minutes."

"Right? I'm starting to worry. She said she would be here about half an hour ago." Nedra reached for her phone, and she nodded her head. "That was her. She's going to be late. Something about a case and a witness she needs to interview today because it's the only day the witness is available."

"Sorry. Will she make it for dinner?"

"I hope so."

Stacy waved to a woman getting out of her car. "Tegan."

The woman waved back as she walked toward the green. She looked familiar, with her light, golden-brown hair, confident stride, and muscular legs.

We all followed Stacy and Marilyn as they greeted the woman with a hug. "I'm glad you could make it," said Marilyn.

"Oh, I'm glad to be here and outside on this beautiful day."

"Everyone, this is Tegan Roberts," Stacy said. "We grew up together and she just moved back into the area. And like me, she's a recently retired teacher."

"Hi. What did you teach?" Nedra asked.

"English."

"What's your handicap?" Cindy asked.

"Oh, I don't know. Pick a number."

Frieda laughed. "I hear you."

Tegan cocked her head to one side as she scrutinized my face. Her eyes were bright hazel and searching. "Do I know you? You look familiar."

I shuffled my feet, and my gaze dropped to the ground before I looked back at her surprised expression. "I believe we crossed paths in Meijer last week. I ran into your grocery cart."

"Ah, yes," she said, realization dawning on her features. "You weren't too happy with me at the time."

Everyone turned to me. I shrugged and turned my palms up. "The cart was in the middle of the aisle at the corner, and I crashed into it and bruised my shin."

"I bet you were on the phone with one of your clients," Marilyn said.

"No. I'd just ended my call with Susan, who told me Scott Wolford had registered a team for today."

"What?" Nedra said.

"Yes, I did," a male voice said behind us.

We all pivoted simultaneously.

"Hello, Dayna," Scott said.

Scott stood tall, his lean frame filling out a matching Izod golf outfit, complete with a visor and white leather shoes that gleamed in the sunlight. His blond hair was grayer, and his eyes softer. Three other people stood beside him, each with a different shade of green, from pale lime to deep emerald, and their expressions were set in determined grins as they waited for whatever was going to happen next. My eyes widened as I recognized them.

"Hello, Scott," I said as Cindy touched my elbow and the others stepped forward on either side of me.

"Dayna, you remember my wife, Meredith, and our two children, Denise and Andrew?"

My breath caught as I took in the familiar faces. "Meredith. Denise, Andrew." I inhaled. Denise, probably in her early twenties, still bore a striking resemblance to Catherine, with her strawberry-blond hair cascading down her shoulders and her athletic figure adorned with high cheekbones. Meanwhile, Andrew, two years younger, had inherited his father's lean frame and blond locks, but his square jawline mirrored Catherine's. And just like Catherine, they both had deep, dark-brown eyes that seemed to hold the same glint of mischievousness.

"Hello, Ms. Baldwin," Andrew said.

"Hello, Dayna," Denise said.

"Meredith, you were separated last time Catherine and I talked to Scott. I assume things worked out?"

"We were separated until about two years ago," Meredith answered.

She had not changed much, as she was still attractive with her auburn hair, alert blue eyes and feminine round cheeks.

"Vonda died two years ago," Scott said.

My body stiffened on hearing the name.

"I understand what she did was unforgivable," Scott said.

"Damn right," Nedra said, stepping forward. "It was more than unforgivable. It was inhumane."

Frieda grabbed Nedra's arm and pulled her back. "Nedra."

"Come on." Nedra turned to us. "You all remember how hurt we were and how devastated Dayna was."

Other golfers slowly walked by us, observing the awkward standoff.

Marilyn stepped forward and directed the golfers. "Please, go right in. The registration table is on the right. Enjoy your day."

I cleared my throat. "Scott, I need to talk to the starter and make sure we're ready for the shotgun start at one." I took a step toward the clubhouse.

I heard Nedra whisper, "Let me at 'em."

Scott turned and followed me as I walked away. His steps echoed behind me, each heavy with the weight of his pleading words. "Dayna, please let me explain. It won't take long."

My muscles coiled like a spring as I came to a stop. Heavy suffocating silence hung between us as I waited for him to resume.

Marilyn walked to my side. "We'll talk to the starter and make sure everything is ready."

"Come on." Frieda waved, and everyone followed Marilyn, holding their putters, with Cindy dragging Nedra by the arm.

I turned to Scott and gave him a stern look. "Talk."

"I'm sorry I wasn't strong enough to confront my mother about you and Catherine. And what she did, preventing you visiting Catherine in the hospital, and the funeral—"

I interrupted and said through gritted teeth, "I remember." I pointed to my chest. "It's right here, what she did. You don't have to tell me."

He looked back at his wife, who nodded in encouragement. "Okay." He held up both hands. "I'll get to the point."

"Please." I clenched my jaw so tightly it hurt.

"My family's company will continue to support your charity golf outing in honor of Catherine. And, if you allow us, my family would like to become more involved."

I looked behind Scott, where his family stood next to each other. Meredith held Denise's hand, and Andrew's hand was on his mother's shoulder. They stood like statues, holding their breath.

I returned my eyes to Scott. His eyes pleaded for an answer.

"I'll have to think about that."

"Dayna, I don't expect you to embrace my family with open arms as if nothing's happened." He stepped back. "But you should know we are serious, all of us"—he gestured to his family—"about wanting to be involved with Catherine's fundraiser for the AHA if you'll allow us."

I sighed. "Your family is your team?"

"Yes."

"Well." I pointed at the door to the pro shop. "You better go sign in and find out what hole you start on."

"Thank you, Dayna." He walked toward the door.

Denise followed. "Thanks, Dayna."

Meredith touched my arm as she passed me. "Thank you, Dayna."

All three walked up the brick path toward the clubhouse.

Andrew stopped next to me. "So, what's your handicap?"

The other three halted and turned, holding their breath.

I turned and stared at Andrew. His eyes were as brown as Catherine's. Vonda's behavior had nothing to do with the children.

"Better than yours." I smiled and slapped his shoulder. Everyone exhaled. "Now get in there and sign in."

CHAPTER SEVENTEEN

"Okay, so Tegan can take Leslie's place with my team," Nedra said. "Frieda and Stacy can exchange teams. That way, Stacy can be with Tegan, and Dayna can give Frieda more golf lessons. Does that work for everyone?"

"Works for me," Frieda said.

Tegan, beside me, said, "I'm happy to be on any team. Thanks, Stacy, for the invite."

"Excuse me?" a blond woman interrupted. "Hi, Dayna." I tilted my head as my brain went through my client list.

"Yes. And you are?" I asked.

"Oh, you don't remember? Victoria Abernathy. Washington, D.C., the conference. I attended your session." She touched my arm. "You showed me how to explode through the glass ceiling."

I took a deep breath as I rubbed the back of my neck.

"Exploding through the glass ceiling?" Nedra asked.

"Oh yes." I gathered myself and tried to act professionally. "You wanted to break the glass ceiling and become a bank president."

Tegan's head swiveled between me, Victoria, and everyone else.

"I just wanted to tell you that I did explode through the ceiling. I'm the new president of Fifth Third Bank in Dayton."

"Congratulations."

"I'm here with some employees." She pointed to a group of three women. "I would like it"—she took a step closer and ran her finger down my arm—"if you would join us after the event for drinks."

I turned from my friends and stepped toward the woman. "Victoria, unfortunately, I have to stay and help clean up."

Victoria stepped back with a smirk. "Well, at least they got you to stay."

"Oh, shit," Frieda mumbled. "One of her one-night stands."

Stacy jumped in. "Dayna, you need to welcome everyone. Why don't we walk you to the microphone?"

Victoria moved within inches of Tegan, who was by my side. "If I were you, don't get too close. She'll fuck you, then leave. She's not one to stay."

I turned to Tegan as heat radiated from my neck. I opened my mouth, but nothing came out. I turned back to Victoria. "Why are you here?"

Victoria moved back from Tegan. "My bank gives back to the community. The board wanted us to contribute to Catherine Wolford's charity, whoever she is."

I jerked forward, as did the others. Tegan grabbed my arm. Cindy jumped between Victoria and me. "Why don't we all take a deep breath, go to our separate corners, and get ready to golf."

Victoria spun on her heel and dashed back to her group, laughing.

"What the hell was that?" Marilyn asked. "One of your one-night stands catching up with you?"

"Fuck it. I have things to do." I walked away, my face flushed.

When the starter used the PA system to ask all golfers to go to their carts, golfers of all genders, races, shapes, and sizes, dressed in every color imaginable, scattered toward their carts. I overheard comments about how beautiful the day was, how far they could drive the ball, and how they were ready to have fun. Catherine would be so proud of the diversity of those attending in her honor.

Marilyn and Tegan caught up with me and walked with me toward the carts. Tegan asked, "You okay?"

I jerked my head. "Like you care? You don't even know me."

"Dayna," Marilyn said.

Tegan's hazel eyes showed compassion. "It appears you had a few unexpected visitors today."

"Yeah, so what? I'll survive like I always do."

"Ladies and gentlemen," the starter began. "I want to introduce the person responsible for this event and ask her to say a few words. Golfers, your host for today's event, Dayna Baldwin."

CHAPTER EIGHTEEN

My feelings of loss accelerated as I stood next to the starter. "Welcome, everyone, to the fourth annual Catherine Wolford Charity Golf Outing for the American Heart Association. Catherine, my life partner, and I had been together for fifteen years when she suddenly died of a heart attack. She had no symptoms or signs of heart issues. However, she left behind a strong group of friends and colleagues who wanted to honor her, and this outing was born to support cardiovascular education programs for women."

Everyone clapped.

I thanked the sponsors and major contributors and informed the golfers that a buffet of chicken wings, hamburgers, brats, and various side dishes would be waiting for them upon completion of their round of golf.

"And how about a big thank you to Beechwood Golf Course for their hospitality," I added. Everyone hooted and hollered.

I searched the four rows of golf carts lined eight deep, two people in a cart, and found Scott and Meredith in a cart with their two children in a cart behind them.

I yelled, "Scott—Scott Wolford. Will you come up and say a few words about your sister?"

Scott's eyes bulged. He glanced at Meredith and his children behind him. Meredith gently pushed Scott out of the cart.

My friends' mouths dropped open. Nedra mouthed, "What the fuck?"

"Scott, Catherine's brother, and his family have joined us today. You'll notice the Wolford Real Estate Company signs on a few holes. His company has committed to supporting this event in the future."

There was more applause as I handed the microphone to Scott, and he mouthed, "Thank you." Scott began, "Thank you, Dayna, and everyone, for joining us today to honor my sister, who..."

I slowly moved toward my cart, glancing up briefly as I passed Meredith, who looked somber. She gently touched my arm, her eyes bright with unshed tears. "Dayna, you should know that Scott has returned to his old self—the husband I fell in love with so many years ago. Catherine's death and the events that followed pushed him to his breaking point, but fortunately, he got help and learned how to stand up to Vonda and challenge how the company was being run. Thank you for showing him this kindness and understanding."

There was a tap on my shoulder. I turned, and Denise looked at me, misty-eyed. She embraced me and whispered, "I remember you." She released me. "I remember you, Catherine, and me taking walks and playing catch. Thank you for giving my dad back his sister."

"I remember too." I wiped my tears. "Thank you for coming today."

Denise turned as I went to my cart. I slumped down into the seat next to Frieda and took a deep breath, putting my forehead in my hands.

Frieda placed her hand on my back. "Why did you do that?"

Marilyn stepped out of her cart behind us and rested her hand on my shoulder.

I straightened up. "Catherine wanted to rekindle her relationship with Scott and his family. She might not have been able to do that while she was alive, but maybe she can in her death."

In the background, Scott said, "Everyone, enjoy yourselves, and thanks again for being here on this beautiful day honoring my sister."

More applause.

The starter said, "The marshals will lead you to your holes. Play well and have fun."

Marilyn returned to her cart, and I stepped on the throttle and drove to the first tee with Nedra's team behind us.

Our team was on the eleventh hole, a dogleg left. My shot bounced once, took another awkward bounce to the left, and settled in the middle of the fairway.

As we parked at my ball for our second shot, our carts hidden from the tee box, Rebecca said, "Frieda, much better shot."

"Okay, we're about a hundred yards from the green. Marilyn, lead the way," Rebecca said.

Marilyn took her shot, followed by Rebecca and Frieda. Marilyn and Rebecca were on the edge of the green, and Frieda was ten yards from it.

"Okay, Dayna. It'll be a hell of a long putt for a birdie if you don't get closer," Marilyn said.

I pulled out my pitching wedge, walked to the ball, and lined up for my shot. A ball rocketed into my butt on my backswing, and the word "fore" echoed through the trees.

I dropped my club. "Ouch. Damn it." I rubbed my butt. "Where did that come from?"

Rebecca pointed. "The tee box."

Stacy and Tegan drove up to us, and Tegan said, "Sorry." Nedra and Cindy joined us and parked next to Stacy and Tegan.

My eyes focused on Tegan. "Don't you know you yell fore as soon as you realize the ball is flying toward people?"

"Dayna," Stacy said.

"Come on. Everyone knows you yell fore. Who doesn't know that etiquette?" I rubbed my butt.

Tegan held back a chuckle. "Is your butt okay?"

I waved my hand and picked up my club.

"Do you need help rubbing your butt?" Tegan asked.

"Really? Do you think this is funny? Your ball could have hit my head and been more serious."

"Dayna." Stacy turned to me. "It was my ball. I forgot to yell, and Tegan yelled for me."

"Oh." I faced Tegan, my head held low. "Sorry."

"And it didn't hit your head, only your ass," Nedra said.

Tegan's eyes gravitated to my butt. "It's a nice ass, if I must say."

Stacy looked at me and smiled.

"You're still talking about my ass, which I'm sure will have a bruise."

Marilyn said, "I'm sure it'll be black and blue."

I chuckled. "Well, since you're so interested." I unbuttoned my shorts and pulled down my zipper. "Why don't we check out how pretty it will be?"

"Dayna!" Frieda yelled. "Don't you dare!" She scampered out of the cart and stepped in front of me so no one would see my butt.

"Got ya." I laughed as the others joined in.

"Okay. Back to golf. I bet we're holding up the people behind us. Come on, back in our carts," Stacy said.

We finished the eleventh hole, moving around the course until we were back in the parking lot, loading our clubs into our cars.

CHAPTER NINETEEN

Nedra's foursome had the lowest score and snagged the women's team award. Frieda was rewarded for the longest putt, and Rebecca won the longest drive for women.

The golfers had dined, collected their prizes, and exited the clubhouse. I walked onto the patio facing the golf course and examined the first green. There was a slight breeze as the sun moved behind the trees, casting a shadow. I smiled and rubbed my butt as I remembered Tegan's comment.

"Dayna!" Frieda skipped to me. "Look at my paperweight for the longest putt! And I get a free round of golf here at Beechwood."

"It was the best putt of the day, and you had the pa—"

"Yeah, yeah, I know, the pace. It's all about the pace."

A small smile tugged at the corners of my lips, a momentary relief from the tension gripping me all day. Frieda's voice cut through my thoughts as I released a long sigh.

"What a day, huh?" she interrupted, her tired expression mirroring mine as we both processed the day. "It was very considerate of you to let Scott say a few words."

"Meredith says he's changed since Catherine's death. That he's back to the man she married."

"I'm glad the family is back together."

I turned to Frieda. "Denise told me she remembers me. She remembers Catherine and me taking walks and playing catch with her."

"How could she not remember? You and Catherine doted over those two."

"Until they kicked us out of the family when the kids were in grade school."

"What's important is that she remembers."

"Catherine would be thrilled."

"She would."

"Hey, you two," Marilyn said, "you ready to go?"

"Are we the only ones left?"

"Yes," Stacy said as she and Tegan joined us.

I noticed Tegan's pink, sleeveless golf polo and black women's golf shorts, showing off her muscular arms and legs.

"Do you like pink?" I asked.

"Why do you ask?"

"When I saw you in Meijer, you wore a pink top."

"Pink is my mom's favorite color. She thinks it should be mine, too."

Stacy chimed in, "Speaking of your mom, Tegan, how is she?"

"Better, thanks for asking. My brothers and I now have a schedule, which gives me more free time on the weekends."

"Maybe you'd like to join our group sometime?" Frieda asked.

"I had a fun time today. So, I would like that—if no one minds me crashing your group," Tegan said, looking directly at me.

We exited the clubhouse and met with Cindy and Leslie, walking toward us. "Come on, everybody. Let's go. Nedra is waiting in the car. She wants to invite you all over for a drink."

"Not tonight," I said. "I'm beat."

"Anyone?"

"Cindy?" Frieda asked.

"Sure, why not? We'll meet you there."

"Not us. We're heading home," Stacy said as she held Marilyn's hand.

"Okay, great job today, Dayna. Sorry, I missed the golfing. But the food was delicious," Leslie said.

"I'm glad you at least got to eat."

We were all parked near each other. I turned to the group. "Thanks, everyone, for being here today. Your support means a lot to me."

"You're welcome. We're always here for you," Marilyn said as they all got in their cars and headed out.

Tegan and I were there alone. When I turned to her, I noticed we were only a couple of feet apart, staring at each other. Her intense eyes sent warmth through me, so I broke eye contact.

"Uh...thanks for joining us today." I hung my head. "And I'm sorry about jumping you about the 'fore' thing."

Tegan's eyes sparkled as she held back a smile.

"What? You want to say something."

"I don't know you well enough to say what I'm thinking."

"Say it anyway."

"It's related to your jumping-me comment."

"Oh, yeah." I bit my lip. "Maybe hold your comment for later."

Tegan held her head high and maintained eye contact with me. "Till later."

"So, back to my apology—"

"Dayna, I assume this day was stressful for you even without the surprise visitors."

"That's kind of you to say, but I'm still sorry."

"Apology accepted."

"Thank you. I hope to see you around."

"I hope so."

We walked toward our separate cars. My head was bowed low, keeping my eyes cast down. I slumped into the driver's seat, resting my head back. Closing my eyes, I breathed deeply before starting the engine. This day was always draining, but today was even more so.

I smiled as I remembered a Thanksgiving when Catherine and I played kickball with Denise and Andrew. The day was crisp and cool, but the sun was bright, and we were all bundled up in fleece coats and hats, scarves, and gloves to fend off the wind. We ran all over Catherine's parents' manicured lawn. It was half a football field of perfectly groomed grass with century-old oak trees looming over it.

Andrew must've been four, and Denise six. Catherine and Andrew had formed a team against Denise and me. On our last turn to kick, Denise and I made a plan with Andrew.

"Okay, Denise, you ready?" Catherine had asked.

"Ready, Aunt Catherine and Andrew?" Denise had said. "Roll the ball and be ready to chase it because it's going way over your heads."

Catherine and I had smiled at each other.

"Here it comes," Catherine had said as she rolled the ball.

Denise took two giant steps, swung her leg at the oncoming ball, and kicked it over their heads. Catherine and Andrew's heads followed the ball, they turned and sprinted after it.

As Denise ran to first base, she yelled, "Now!"

Andrew grabbed Catherine's leg and hung on for dear life.

"Andrew, what are you doing?" Catherine asked, looking down at Andrew, who grinned from ear to ear. That was when she'd noticed Denise, who had taken a sharp left turn and was running toward her.

"I got her," Andrew had yelled.

"We're coming," Denise had said, sprinting toward Catherine and grabbing her other leg.

"What is this? This is kickball, not football," Catherine had said with a smile.

I followed Denise and grabbed Catherine around her waist as we all fell to the ground, laughing.

I smiled and shook my head to bring myself back to reality. Denise said she remembered.

I put my car in reverse and backed out as the sun set. Tegan got out of her car as I passed. I stopped and hung my head out the window. "Something wrong?"

"The damn thing won't start."

"Does it do that often?"

"No. It sounds like the battery is dead. And I need to get home."

I parked beside her and asked her to start it again. I listened to the clicking sound. "Yep, that sounds like the battery to me, too." I got out and walked toward her with a smile.

She looked at me with one eyebrow raised. "I have jumper cables. Will you jump me?"

We looked at each other, our eyes wide, and laughed heartily until tears ran down our faces.

"Oh, I needed that," I said.

"I'm glad I can help." Tegan reached into her trunk and grabbed the cables.

I reached out to her. "Why don't you give me the cables while you pop your hood?"

Tegan sat in the driver's seat with one foot in and the other on the ground, and popped the hood. She stepped out of the car, and I handed her one end of the cable and kept the other. We connected the cables to the batteries, and she returned to the car. "Here goes." She turned the ignition and the car started.

I pumped my fists in the air. "Success."

Tegan stepped out of the car as I removed the cables. "Thank you."

"No problem. I'm glad I was here to help."

When I handed the cables back to her, our hands touched. A jolt of electricity shot up my arm, and my heart skipped a beat.

I heard Tegan inhale and felt her hesitate as she stared at our hands. Finally, she exhaled, and returned them to her trunk. On her way back to the driver's side door, she stopped. "Thank you for your help and the laugh."

"I'm sure you'd do the same. Drive safe."

"You too," Tegan said as she hopped into her car. As her rear lights faded into the sunset, I touched my hand, remembering.

CHAPTER TWENTY

Two weeks after the golf outing, Marilyn called and asked if she could stop by on her way home from work. The Ohio humidity kept me indoors, so I was making freshly squeezed lemonade in the kitchen when the doorbell rang, and Marilyn came in. I handed her a glass of lemonade. "Here, let's sit and relax."

Marilyn and I sat on the leather couch. "We haven't seen you since the golf outing. Every time we call to ask you to go out, you say you're busy. What's up with that?"

"It took me a while to recover."

Marilyn took a long drink. "I can imagine why with the surprise guests who showed up."

I shrugged my shoulders and smiled.

"What's that smile about?"

"Nothing. I think I slept till noon on that Sunday. After that, all I did all day was lounge around the house."

"You should have come down and lounged in our pool," Marilyn said, avoiding eye contact with me.

"I know we only live a mile from each other, but—" Marilyn had been Catherine's closest friend and business partner. Now that I wasn't part of a couple, figuring out how I fit into the group was challenging.

"Come on, Dayna. You're always welcome."

"Yeah, I know. You drank that pretty fast. You need a refill?"

"No, I'm good. Thanks."

Marilyn's hand trembled as she turned the glass of water in her fingers. A nervous energy radiated off her, causing her to fidget and tap her feet.

My stomach twisted anxiously as I watched her. "Is everything okay?"

She took a deep breath before setting the glass on the coffee table, and leaned forward to speak. "I need to tell you something about the business." Her voice shook slightly.

I leaned back onto the couch and braced myself.

Marilyn turned to me. "I'm thinking about retiring and selling to Rebecca."

"Okay. I thought it was something serious." I grabbed her arm. "Congratulations!"

We'd benefited financially from Catherine's partnership with Marilyn in the real estate business, which allowed us to create beautiful vacation memories and connect with lifelong friends. Catherine and I often discussed business and problem-solved management issues together. But when she died, I stepped back from my involvement with her company. I missed those discussions, but my consulting business had filled that gap.

"Marilyn, we talked about this after Catherine died. You and Catherine had legal documents that would allow the surviving party to gain full control of the company if something happened to one of you. I was happy to honor her agreement because that's what she would've wanted. So, you, my friend, are an honorable steward of the company, and bringing Rebecca on as a partner was insightful."

"I know. She's smart and hardworking and quickly learned the ins and outs of the real estate business."

I straightened my posture and made direct eye contact with Marilyn. "Then the company will be in worthy hands." I changed the subject. "Now, when is your retirement date? And what about the wedding?"

"We're finalizing the contracts as we speak, and the process should be complete within a few weeks."

"And the wedding? Last time we talked, I think you said sometime in the fall."

"We're looking at a date in September. Just a few months away." Marilyn smiled. "The wedding will be with our friends and family at our house, in the yard."

"So, you and Stacy will be the first to have a date to tie the knot."

"Yeah, we want to coordinate the wedding with my retirement so we can take a long vacation, or I guess you could call it our honeymoon, but we've been together for over thirty years."

"Wow! Time flies."

"So, now that we will both be retired, it will be a vacation where we stay as long as we want without worrying about answering emails or returning phone calls. Just relaxing. No deadlines. No worries. Just relaxing."

"If you need help with the wedding, please don't hesitate to ask."

"Oh, don't worry. We will. I better get going. Stacy is probably waiting on me for dinner."

"Thanks for stopping by and telling me all of this." She opened the door, and I followed her onto the front porch. "See ya later. Hi to Stacy."

"We're having a few friends over on Saturday. Want to join us?"

"Sure. What time?"

"Any time after one. Nedra will be grilling chicken for dinner."

"Want me to bring anything?"

"Just yourself." Marilyn waved as she entered her car.

As the birds chirped merrily in the pine trees surrounding my house, I stood on the porch and watched Marilyn turn down the road. The warm air and the lazy breeze brought me a hint of comfort. I closed my eyes momentarily and imagined Catherine sitting on a bench, her head on my shoulder as we listened to the birds' song. Would Catherine have been retired by now? Would we have been planning our wedding? Marilyn and Stacy were moving on with their lives. Would I move forward or stay in that comfortable nostalgic place?

CHAPTER TWENTY-ONE

I twirled around, and my smile widened as I examined the reflection in the full-length mirror. The purple of my tankini top caught the light and shimmered with each turn. I tugged at the black bottoms, feeling a thrill of satisfaction as they hugged my curves and hid any hint of a belly bulge. Smiling, I smoothed down my hair, gave myself a pep talk, and grabbed my tote containing a towel, a change of clothes, sunscreen, and sunglasses. Adjusting my sun visor, I headed out the door.

"Dayna! I'm so glad to see you," Stacy said as she greeted me.

I set my tote on the ground by the picnic table, next to all the others. She hugged me. "Thanks, it's good to be here." I grabbed my towel and sunscreen and slipped on my sunglasses.

She put her arm around me and squeezed. "Come on. Everyone's by the pool."

We stepped through the gate of the six-foot iron fence enclosing the pool area. Black lounge chairs and straight-backed chairs were scattered on the pool deck. The pool's dark-blue lining and bright sunlight reflecting off the clear water beckoned me.

In her usual black one-piece and straw hat that blocked the sun, Marilyn sat on the deck, her legs hanging in the water. Frieda and Cindy waved from the double-seated float, wearing sunglasses and broad-rimmed sun hats.

Frieda said, "Hey, Dayna. We've missed you."

I reached my hands to the blue sky. "I'm back among the living."

"Well, I should say so, with your suit," Cindy said. "I love the color."

"Thanks, and it covers my belly." I laughed.

"We all have 'em," Frieda said.

"More to love," Cindy said as she reached and laid her hand on Frieda's belly.

"Where are the others?" I asked.

"Nedra and Leslie are in the house, finalizing the appetizers they brought," Marilyn said.

"Yeah," Stacy said, "but that was forty-five minutes ago."

I opened my towel and laid it over the black iron chair, my visor and sunglasses on the black iron table beside the chair. The umbrella blocked most of the sunshine.

"Ready or not, here I come," I yelled as I jumped and did a cannonball by Frieda and Cindy. I popped up, and water dripped from the rims of their sun hats, and their raft rocked in the waves. Frieda wiped water from her eyes.

"You are the best cannonballer. We needed to be cooled off anyway," Cindy said, then splashed me.

I turned onto my back and floated, blocking all thoughts from my mind.

Ten minutes later, Nedra carried the appetizers to the two round tables. She sported her usual skimpy, bright-orange bikini, and Leslie was in a black one-piece Speedo.

Leslie pointed. "Chips and dip, grilled pineapple salsa, and cheesy corn poppers."

"Sounds delicious," I said.

Frieda and Cindy paddled their way to the side of the pool, and Marilyn handed them a plate full of appetizers. They shoved off the poolside and returned to floating, the afternoon sun baking them.

"I'm ready for a dip in the pool," Nedra said. She took off her bikini top and dove in.

Leslie shrugged. "Sorry. I can't control her."

"That's typical Nedra. Nothing new," Marilyn said.

Nedra resurfaced at the other end of the pool. "Ahh. So refreshing."

"Anyone up for volleyball?" Stacy asked.

Marilyn and Stacy stretched a volleyball net across the length of the pool. We passed a rainbow beach ball back and forth over the net. Of course, the shorter people stayed in the shallow end while the taller people were directed to the deeper end, making jumping harder.

There was much laughter and splashing, and voices called, "Mine."

"Yours."

"What was *that*?"

"Bring it on."

"That was mine."

"Got it!"

I jumped, faked a pass, and directed the ball into an uncovered spot on the opposite side of the net.

"Nice shot," someone said.

I glanced toward the voice, water running down my face. At the top of the steps stood Tegan, leaning against the handrail.

Our eyes locked.

She wore a blue, two-toned, skirted one-piece. Her hair was pulled back into a ponytail.

Water bombarded me from all sides. I covered my face.

"Earth to Dayna," Nedra laughed.

"Okay. Stop."

"Glad you made it, Tegan," Stacy said.

"Sorry, I'm late. It's a delicate operation looking after Mom. My brother arrived late. His wife's car wouldn't start, so they had to scramble for another ride to get to their daughter's softball game."

"No worries. Glad you're here," Cindy said as she waved her hand. "Come on in. The water feels great."

My eyes followed Tegan as she placed her towel on the nearest chair, her olive skin shimmering in the sunlight. The back of her one-piece suit clung to her like a second skin, showcasing her pert buttocks as she gracefully made her way toward the pool's steps. She grabbed the handrail, and the water slowly swallowed her ankles, calves, thighs, and hips.

My stomach tightened.

"Be on our team," Cindy said. "Dayna, you go on the other team."

I dove under the net and stood as Tegan walked past me. Her high cheekbones and defined jawline showed off her hazel eyes. Her hand brushed my thigh under the water.

She turned. "Sorry."

When we were across from each other, our eyes linked in a never-ending stare, silently conveying thoughts and emotions.

Finally, Tegan glanced at Nedra. "Do you always play volleyball topless?"

"I do, but the others are too shy. Does it bother you? I can put on my top."

"Doesn't bother me," Tegan said as she smiled at Nedra.

"Oh. I like her."

"Serve the damn ball, Nedra," Leslie said.

Nedra served and we continued our game for another thirty minutes. Tegan moved gracefully, positioned herself to receive a pass, and directed her shot an inch out of my reach.

My body ascended out of the water and slammed back into the water. I stood. "Nice shot."

"Learned it from you," Tegan said with a smile that made my stomach flip.

I dipped under the water, then emerged and wiped my face. "I'm done. I need a break," I said.

"Me too," said Stacy.

"Yeah, I think we all need a break. My skin is like a prune," Frieda said.

I swam under the net until I reached the steps. Holding onto the handrail, I stumbled on the top step, hitting my ankle.

A hand grabbed my hip. "You okay?" Tegan asked.

I turned. Tegan was right beside me. My hip was on fire from her touch.

"Uh, yeah. Thanks. The steps are slippery."

"By the way, good to see you again." She removed her hand, and the fire was smothered.

"Yeah. Good to see you too."

We walked side by side to the chair where our towels were next to each other, and I asked as I grabbed mine and threw it over my shoulders, "Did you get your battery checked? Did you need a new one?"

"Yes, and yes." She smiled. "I bought a new one, and it purrs like a cat. Thanks again for 'jumping' me." She made air quotes when she said jumping.

I chuckled and blushed. "I'm not going to live that one down, am I?"

"You're just easy to tease."

If you only knew.

CHAPTER TWENTY-TWO

After munching on appetizers, I jumped on a sky-blue float and drifted across the pool. Frieda and Cindy were back to floating while Leslie and Nedra sank into the lounge chairs, soaking up the sun's now-gentle rays. Marilyn and Stacy sat on the pool's edge, letting their legs dip into the cool water. Tegan, on another blue float, drifted alongside me.

As she took a deep breath, her chest rose and fell, causing the fabric of her suit to cling to her curves. Our height difference was noticeable as her feet rested on the float while my feet hung off the edge. Her delicate, manicured hands rested on her taut stomach. I couldn't help but notice the fine lines around her lips and eyes, adding character to her otherwise flawless face.

My eyes traced down to her shapely hips and toned legs. The mere thought of her climbing on top of me sent a jolt of excitement through my body.

Tegan placed her hand on my float and touched my arm. "You awake?"

I quickly averted my gaze, almost causing my sunglasses to fly off my face. "Yeah."

"How have you been? You recuperated from the golf outing?"

"Yeah."

Her hand remained on my arm.

"Any new surprises in your life?"

"No."

She squeezed my arm. "Talkative, aren't you." And squeezed my arm again.

Frieda asked, "Any updates on weddings?"

All eyes turned to Leslie and Nedra, holding hands between the lounge chairs, Nedra bare-breasted.

"Any wedding updates?" Frieda asked more loudly.

I plopped off my float, swam to the pool's edge, and splashed Leslie and Nedra.

They both bolted up and said in unison, "Hey."

Nedra asked, "You talking to us?"

"Duh. Yes."

Leslie smiled and grabbed Nedra's hand. "We're planning a December wedding at my parents' house in Columbus. They are so excited to share this with us."

"Ohhh. That's wonderful," Frieda said.

"I hate to interrupt, but I'm getting hungry," Stacy announced.

"Okay, I can take a hint," Nedra said. "I'll start the chicken."

As Nedra pulled herself off the chair, Leslie added, "And please put on a top to grill. I don't want anything to happen to—"

Nedra stood and interrupted as she lifted her breasts. "To your aphrodisiacs?"

"Nedra," Frieda said. "Please."

"Oh, you love it, Frieda. Look at you blush," Nedra teased.

Nedra grabbed a bright-yellow T-shirt and made her way toward the grill. Stacy and Tegan offered to help.

My eyes stayed glued to Tegan as she slid off her float and swam gracefully to the steps. Her hips and ponytail swayed with each step out of the pool. I breaststroked toward Marilyn in the pool's shallow end. I glanced toward Tegan and Stacy, who had stopped and turned to look at me. Both giggled and took the steps into the house.

"We noticed you giving Tegan the once-over," Marilyn said.

"Me? Nooo." I shook my head, sending droplets of water and my sunglasses flying.

"Come on, Dayna. Just because you have sunglasses doesn't mean no one sees you ogling her."

Like a missile, I sprang out of the water. "I am not."

"Calm down." Marilyn touched my arm. "It's about time someone got your attention."

"I am not ogling her."

Frieda and Cindy both said, "Yes. You are."

I spun around to face my friends, then turned back to Marilyn. I let out a low groan before submerging myself beneath the water. At the bottom of the pool, I squeezed my head between my hands in despair. I jumped up, and their laughter filled the air.

I walked toward the steps and changed the subject. "Looks like this will be the year of weddings." When I reached the top step, I turned to Frieda and Cindy. "So, when is yours?"

They turned to each other, and Cindy said, "Next year. Maybe in the spring."

"Chicken is on the grill," Nedra yelled.

CHAPTER TWENTY-THREE

Nedra carried the chicken to the picnic table, where the side dishes of macaroni salad, baked parmesan zucchini, and creamy mashed potatoes awaited.

"Okay," Marilyn said, "dinner's ready. Grab a plate."

I got in line behind Frieda. She put a spoonful of macaroni salad on her plate and asked, "Dayna, do you have any free time to golf?"

"Maybe. What day and time are you thinking?" I placed two chicken legs on my plate.

"Well, since I won the free golf round at the charity outing, I'd like to use it before the end of summer. It is August, so I was hoping next weekend—Saturday or Sunday."

I filled my plate with mashed potatoes. "I think I'll be in town, so yeah, I'd like that."

"Great. Now we need to find two more people," she said as we sat next to each other at the table.

We waited for Cindy, the last in line, to sit as my mind went back to 2009 when Catherine collapsed just a few feet from this table.

Someone said, "Ready?"

Marilyn continued, "Everyone has something to drink?" She raised her glass of Pepsi and said, "To family."

We all followed suit and clinked glasses, saying in unison, "To family."

I scanned the group and remembered when this tradition began years ago after we all vacationed in Topsail Beach, North Carolina. It had led to watching Monday Night Football, which led to celebrating birthdays and anniversaries, supporting each other through knee replacements, bitching about hot flashes, helping each other move into new homes, crying together at sad movies, more vacations and supporting each other as we lost loved ones and parents. I was grateful for this family, which cradled me with love when I had needed it the most.

"Hey, Dayna, not hungry?" Stacy asked.

"What?"

"You haven't touched your chicken."

"Ah, yeah, I'm hungry." I grabbed a leg. "I'm just daydreaming." I took a bite, then said, "Nedra, great job as usual."

Our conversation led to soccer.

"Okay, how about the US Women's World Cup win over Japan last month?" Frieda said.

Stacy pumped her hand in the air. "Wasn't that great?"

Near the end of dinner, Frieda asked, "Does anyone want to join Dayna and me this weekend for a round of golf?"

Tegan leaned back in her chair, made eye contact with me, and smiled.

Marilyn responded, "Stacy and I are spending the weekend in Columbus with old college friends."

"Why aren't you golfing with Frieda?" Marilyn asked Cindy.

"I have a workshop in Kentucky."

Nedra wiggled her eyebrows. "Oh. A kink workshop?"

Frieda elbowed her. "Stop."

"Actually, yes."

Nedra rubbed her hands together. "Tell me more."

Tegan leaned forward in her chair. "Yes, tell us more."

I looked at Tegan and chimed in, "Yeah, tell us more."

"Well, it's a workshop by the National Coalition for Sexual Freedom, of which I'm a member, and as I told you before, I'm a KAP. The workshop focuses on depathologizing sadism, masochism, cross-dressing, and fetishes and the declassification of kink as a mental health disorder."

"Well, I, for one, agree with that decision," Tegan said.

Everyone at the table turned to her.

"Really?" I stared into her eyes. "Tell us more."

"Well." She cleared her throat. "I believe if two consenting adults want to do whatever to pleasure each other, then"—she looked squarely at me—"why shouldn't they be able to embrace that pleasure? Without being viewed or labeled as abnormal?"

Cindy jabbed her finger in Tegan's direction. "Right. You got it."

"Okay, don't get Cindy started," Frieda said. "Enough about kink and pleasure. Can we get back to my question about golfing this weekend?"

Nedra walked behind Leslie, placing her hands on her shoulders. "Would you like to join me in the pool for some pleasure?"

Leslie slowly shook her head. "Thanks, guys. Now see what you've done."

Nedra raised her hands. "Okay, okay. I'll have to wait till we get back to our place." She kissed Leslie's head and collected the dirty plates, knives, and forks.

"Here, let me help," Tegan said, collecting glasses. Everyone pitched in to clear the tables.

"Thanks, everyone, for your help," Stacy said as we sat back at the table.

"I had a great time today," Tegan said. "Thanks for asking me."

Frieda stood and put her hands on her hips. "So, no one wants to golf with Dayna and me next weekend? It's supposed to be a nice weekend in the high seventies—probably one of the cooler days in August."

Tegan looked at Frieda and then at me. I leaned toward her and smiled wistfully as I bounced my leg.

"I'd love to," Tegan said and then winked at me.

"I'll join you," Nedra said. "Leslie has to work this weekend, preparing for a big case, so I'm in."

Frieda clapped her hands. "Great. I'll schedule the tee time for Saturday at ten. Does that work for everyone?"

We all nodded.

"So, let's meet at Dayna's on Saturday at..." Frieda placed her finger under her chin. "At 9:00 a.m.? Your house is closest on the way to the course, so that should give us enough time to get there."

"We need to get going," Leslie said. "It's getting late." She turned to the group. "Thanks for a great day, everyone."

Cindy said, "Us too. Marilyn and Stacy, thanks for everything. And Nedra, delicious food as always."

Nedra said, "I never pass up spending time with all of you and grilling."

"Oh, we forgot to tell you," Stacy said as she wrapped her arm around Marilyn's waist. "Marilyn and I have picked a date for our wedding."

Everyone turned toward the couple anxiously as Cindy asked, "When?"

"The last Saturday in September, September twenty-sixth," Marilyn said.

"How can we help?" Frieda asked.

I slowly reached the picnic table, collected my tote, and turned toward my car in the gravel driveway.

"All you have to do is show up. It'll be here at four thirty in the afternoon, followed by a catered buffet. We'll be sending out invites next week," Marilyn said.

"The ceremony will be in the side yard, so there will only be twenty people," Stacy added.

I looked down at the pavers leading to the driveway.

"Oh, it will be so wonderful," Frieda said.

Someone came and touched my elbow.

I turned and looked at the delicately manicured hand on my elbow. I raised my head and gazed into Tegan's astute hazel eyes. I glanced back to the others, the ground, and then Tegan. "Sneaking out without a goodbye?"

I overheard Marilyn's response to Frieda's comment. "Well, it should be, as you are the officiant for the ceremony."

"Oh, yeah, I am, aren't I," Frieda said and laughed.

Tegan turned to the group, her hand still on my elbow, and said, "I'm sure it will be lovely."

The group turned toward Tegan and me, and Cindy asked, "You two leaving without a hug?"

I glanced at Marilyn, back down to the spot on the ground, and back to Marilyn.

Marilyn walked to me, hugged me, and whispered, "We all miss her." As she released me, she turned to Tegan. "Thanks for joining us today. You're a good addition to our group."

"Thank you. Stacy told me you're a special group, and she's right."

Tegan picked up her tote and returned to the group for goodbye hugs. I followed and did the same. Walking together to our cars, I said, "See you next Saturday."

"Oh, can you give me your address?"

I stopped. "Oh, yeah. What's your phone number?" I grabbed my phone from my tote. "I'll text it to you, and then you'll have my number, too."

"Sounds good." Tegan's phone dinged. "Got it. Thanks. See you next Saturday." She turned to her car but stopped. "Can I give you a hug?"

My body didn't move as my mind said, *no, don't do it*, but the word "Yes" came out of my mouth.

Tegan took two steps toward me, wrapped an arm around my shoulder, and gave me a one-armed hug as her tote blocked our bodies from touching. "If you ever want to talk about what was on your mind back there, I'm a good listener."

I stepped away from her, my gaze drawn to her mesmerizing eyes. "Thanks, but I'm fine," I replied before darting to my car.

CHAPTER TWENTY-FOUR

I drove the short distance to my house, overwhelmed by emotion as I replayed Tegan's comment, her soft touch, and her comforting hug. I struggled between wanting to learn more about Tegan and feeling like I was betraying Catherine's memory. I slammed the car door shut and rushed inside.

Dropping my tote on the floor, I plodded over to the living room couch and threw myself onto its cushions. I grabbed my phone in my pocket and saw a notification of a missed call. My grip tightened, and tension built in my shoulders as I listened to a message from Denise Wolford. Her voice trembled, and she asked if she could talk to me. She asked me to call her.

I released the breath I'd been holding, and I headed straight to my office. Tapping away at my keyboard, I immersed myself in work to avoid thinking about Tegan, Catherine, kink, and Denise. I responded to emails, made notes of calls to be returned, updated my calendar, and updated notes into client files. I glanced down at the computer clock. It read 10:45. I shut off my computer and walked back toward the living room.

I stepped into my bedroom doorway, flicked on the overhead light. I turned down my oak, mission-style king-sized bed's gray pebbled quilt and matching gray sheets. I switched off the overhead light and turned on one of the industrial-style lamps on the oak nightstand, which glinted invitingly from its top, before heading to the bathroom.

I turned off the bathroom light and strolled toward the bed. As I wrapped the cool, cotton sheet around me, its gentle embrace comforted my bare skin. It served as a shield against the emptiness and loneliness that filled my heart but also stirred a yearning for something more.

CHAPTER TWENTY-FIVE

My Thursday six p.m. Zoom call with Janet, a construction company project manager, ended with me confirming her strategy to approach her superiors about becoming more diverse in their recruitment and hiring practice.

"I've got this. Thanks, Dayna," Janet said.

"Yes, you do. Have a good evening." And we signed off.

I documented the session and shut down my computer. I locked my office door and mentally contemplated tomorrow's schedule and what I had to do for next Tuesday's trip to Cleveland. I'd have time after my three o'clock appointment to go to Meijer and pick up a few items for my trip.

I stopped in front of the refrigerator, turned, and reflected on my house. It was so quiet. The only sound was a battery-operated clock on the kitchen wall and the refrigerator's hum. I scanned its sparse contents for what I could scavenge for dinner: milk, orange juice, and one small can of Diet Sprite. I moved sweet pickles and mayo jars and found leftover spaghetti from dinner two nights ago. I dished it onto a plate and shoved it into the microwave.

As I leaned against the counter, waiting for the *ding* to signal my dinner was ready, I pulled my phone from my back pocket and scanned for new messages. I recognized Denise's phone number from the other night.

I hit the Play button and listened.

"Dayna, it's Denise again. I would really like to talk with you." Sigh. She said confidently, "I would like to speak with you, and after we talk, I will not contact you again. I promise." Then her voice cracked. "Please, for Catherine's sake, can we talk? I hope to hear from you."

I gathered my dinner and sat on the two-person fabric bench at the dinner table. I placed my phone next to my plate, and I thought to myself between bites. I'd survived Catherine's death and Vonda's retribution. I guessed I would survive talking with Denise even though she was a reminder of what was taken from me. I smiled. My therapist would have probably told me it would be a healthy move on my part.

CHAPTER TWENTY-SIX

The sound of '80s pop music filled the air as I approached Meijer's health and beauty aisle, and paused in front of the travel section. I grabbed deodorant and toothpaste and tossed them into my cart, already filled with vegetables, bread, and sandwich meat.

I dodged shopping carts as I moved to the digestive aisle, searching for Colace.

"Dayna?"

My head snapped, and my heart jumped at seeing Tegan and her mom.

"Hi, Dayna," Tegan said with a smile. "Funny meeting you here."

The older woman looked at me curiously and asked, "Who is that?"

Tegan glanced at me. "A friend," she said before she returned to her mother and patted her arm reassuringly. "Mom, wait here. I'll be back in a minute."

The swooshing sound of her sneakers against the tile floor echoed down the aisle as she dashed toward me. We both reached for the same box of Colace before our eyes met in surprise. My cheeks grew hot in embarrassment, so I covered my face with my hands before peeking at Tegan.

Her smile was like a sudden beam of sunlight, melting away all my embarrassment. I smiled back guilt-free.

We turned back toward her mom only to find that she had disappeared. Tegan's expression shifted from worry to panic as she sprinted down the aisle to locate her mother.

I followed closely behind her, but there was no sign of her or the cart. "What's wrong? She probably just finished shopping while we were talking," I murmured in confusion.

Tegan looked me in the eye with desperation etched across her features. "No. She has mild Alzheimer's."

I gently touched Tegan's arm, reassuring her that I'd help her look for her mother. "What's her name?"

"Beti," she whispered, her head swiveling as she searched the adjacent aisle. "I'll go to the right, and you to the left." She nodded before dashing off toward the women's clothing section.

I marched through the store, past sporting goods and automotive supplies, and eventually into the pet section. Beti stood, meticulously selecting cans of dog food from the shelves and placed them in her cart. Swiftly texting Tegan that I'd found her mother, I inserted myself beside Beti and asked if she had a dog.

She spun slowly around to face me. Her hair was darker than Tegan's, but her strong cheekbones and jawline were unmistakable.

"Yes." Beti beamed. "I have a Boston terrier named Queenie." Her eyes glimmered with pride as she recounted how old Queenie was and asked if I had a dog.

Before I responded, Tegan was by my side. "Mom? Do we need dog food?"

Beti turned to me with a motherly smile. "Tegan, this nice person was asking me about Queenie. You know everyone should have a dog."

Tegan smiled at me knowingly as she grabbed her mom's hand and gently steered the cart away from the pet aisle. With her free hand, she gestured for me to follow. We went to the store's back wall, to the dairy section.

Tegan asked her mom to get a carton of milk, and as soon as Beti was out of earshot, Tegan touched my arm and softened her voice. "Thank you for humoring my mom with Queenie. She's been dealing with memory issues for a while. Most people don't understand and try to correct her instead of letting her remember."

I squeezed her hand in understanding. "It was nice meeting your mom. There is no need to thank me."

Tegan forced a smile. At that moment, Beti returned with a gallon of milk and placed it in the cart.

Her mom furrowed her brows. "Why do we have dog food in the cart? Queenie died. Right?"

Without speaking, Tegan pulled Beti close and hugged her tightly.

I draped my arm over their shoulders and felt the warmth of our connection as I reassured them, "We all have our days."

Beti briefly pressed her hand to mine in thanks. Tina Turner's "What's Love Got to Do with It" filled the store. Tegan's eyes met mine as she said to her mother, "Oh, by the way, Mom, this is Dayna. She's the friend I'm golfing with tomorrow. Remember I told you I'm golfing tomorrow?"

"Ah, yes. And your brother is coming by while you're golfing."

"That's right."

Stepping away from Beti, I replied, "Look. I need to go, find my cart, and finish shopping."

"Thanks again." Tegan squeezed my arm.

"Nice to meet you, Dayna," Beti said.

As I turned away, I heard Beti. "We need milk."

CHAPTER TWENTY-SEVEN

Rays of sunshine escaped through white, fluffy clouds drifting across the sky as I loaded my golf bag into the back of my silver Toyota Highlander. A chilly breeze covered my skin. I wondered how long Tegan had been dealing with her mom's Alzheimer's. The tall green cornstalks across the road had been cut to stubble, affording me the scene of the red barn and the tall, silver wind pump turning lazily in a circle.

I inhaled and exhaled the cool morning air. I pondered how Tegan must feel helpless watching her mother lose her faculties, realizing there was little she could do to stop its progression. I could relate to those feelings of helplessness and frustration, so I closed my eyes and prayed like Frieda, calling the Heavenly Creator. "Give Tegan the strength to deal with her mom and comfort her, knowing she is a loving daughter."

Nedra and Frieda had arrived and were loading their golf bags into my car. A blue Honda Civic parked in the driveway. Tegan waved through the front window, and stepped out. "Good morning, everyone. I'm not late, am I?"

Frieda looked at her watch. "Nope, right on time."

I met Tegan at the rear of her car as she unlatched the trunk. "Good morning. Let me help you with your bag."

I lifted her bag from the trunk, and Tegan touched my arm. "Thank you."

"No problem." I piled her clubs in the back of my car.

As Frieda and Nedra slipped into the back seat, I glanced at Tegan. She looked up at the sky as the clouds dissipated and the sun shone onto her face. "It's going to be a good day," she said as she jumped into the passenger seat.

I told myself I'd do everything possible to make it so.

As Nedra expounded on a case of a lesbian couple wanting to adopt twin girls, we rode the thirty-five minutes to the course. I touched Tegan's arm during Nedra's passionate commentary. "How's your mom?"

Tegan glanced at my hand and covered it with her own. "This morning, she's doing better. Thanks for asking." Then she removed her hand.

"Glad to hear it," I said as I turned onto Route 503.

At the course, Nedra and I checked in and drove the carts to the car.

"Okay," Frieda said, "Dayna, you and Tegan take a cart, and Nedra and I will golf together."

I looked at Tegan, who nodded, and I said, "Fine with us."

I asked Tegan, "Do you prefer to drive or ride?"

Tegan smiled. "It depends on who I'm with."

I gazed into her eyes. "Today, you're with me, so what do you prefer?"

"Um, what do you prefer?" Tegan asked as she removed her clubs from the car.

I swallowed hard and set my clubs down. "I'll do whatever you want."

Tegan grinned and grabbed her bag. "Good to know." She placed her clubs behind the driver's side of the cart seat, strapped them in, and jumped behind the steering wheel.

I followed and hooked my clubs in behind the passenger-side seat. I grabbed the safety bar, swung into the seat, and glanced at Tegan as Frieda yelled from behind us, "Let's get this party started."

We maneuvered our carts to the first hole, and everyone but Tegan drove straight up the fairway. Tegan finished the hole with a double bogey and the three of us with a bogey. The second hole was the same, except for Nedra, who parred.

Tegan continued to slice the ball. When she placed the ball on her tee at hole five and lined up her shot, I walked to the tee box. "Would you mind some feedback about your swing?"

Tegan turned with relief in her eyes. "Please. Yes."

"You're not transferring your weight or using your hips."

Nedra said from her cart, "Yeah, hips make all the difference."

Frieda elbowed Nedra in her side.

I looked back to Tegan. "Ignore her and take a practice swing."

I stood behind her as she took a practice swing. My eyes roamed over her well-set shoulders, curvy hips, and muscular thighs and calves.

"Okay, you need to turn your hips more."

Tegan glanced over her shoulder. "I don't understand."

"Okay, set up for your drive. Good—you have the ball off the inside of your left foot." I continued to move my eyes over her body, inspecting her stance. "Your feet are a little wider than your shoulders—good." I walked around and was in front of her. "Grip, good." I walked behind her. "May I touch your hips?"

Tegan glanced over her left shoulder, and her eyes sparkled. "Yes."

Nedra yelled, "Her hips, Dayna. Don't let those hands wander."

I turned and glared at Nedra as Frieda said, "Nedra. Stop."

"I'm showing her how to move her hips to improve her golf swing."

I heard a chuckle from Tegan.

Nedra grinned. "Whatever you say."

I turned. Tegan looked over her shoulder with a suggestive leer, shaking her hips.

I glared at her. "Stop." I swallowed hard and placed my hands on her hips before telling her, "Now start your swing, keeping your left arm straight." As she started her swing, I pushed her left hip to the right and pulled her right hip back, and when she reached the top of her backswing, I said, "Stop and hold this position."

She stopped with her hips turned, her left shoulder pointed down, and her left arm straight.

My hands were still on her hips. "Now, do you feel how your hips have turned?"

"Yes."

I removed my hands, and Tegan lowered her club. "Now, line up and take your shot."

My heart skipped as I backpedaled off the tee box. Tegan set up, swung, and sent the ball barreling straight down the fairway.

"Great shot," Frieda cheered.

Tegan pumped her fist in the air. "I've never hit a ball so well." She walked to me, and her arms engulfed me. "Thanks, Dayna."

I hugged her back. Our bodies fit together like puzzle pieces, and I held on to her longer than necessary. Then I stepped back, keeping my eyes fixed on her. "Now, remember that feeling."

Tegan stepped back. Her hands gently skimmed my arms, and her club dangled from one hand as she stared into my eyes. "Oh, I plan to."

Nedra yelled, "Okay, you two, back in the cart. We don't have all day."

As we approached the next hole, I asked Tegan, "How did you and Stacy meet?"

Tegan explained that they grew up together and attended kindergarten through high school. Stacy attended Miami University, and she went to Eastern Kentucky. They stayed in touch and usually got together during breaks.

As she talked, I fixated on her mouth. Her full lips and white teeth were intoxicating. I imagined how her teeth could ignite the fire in my body.

We exited the cart and took our tee shots at the eleventh hole. Back in the cart, we continued our discussion. "After college?"

Tegan explained that Stacy got a job locally while she took a job in Oregon because she wanted to do something out of her comfort zone and try something new.

Frieda set up for her shot, and Tegan said, "Show us how it's done."

She turned and gave us a thumbs-up. Then she lined up her shot and swung, and the ball landed in front of the green.

We drove to Tegan's ball, and her shot landed two feet from the pin. We all clapped, and Frieda said, "Sign her up for the LPGA."

Tegan returned to the cart. "I should have never told you about your hips," I said.

"Well, I, for one, am glad you did." Tegan touched my thigh. "I especially enjoyed the individual, hands-on instructions."

As we rode to the next hole, I asked Tegan how her mother was doing and she explained she had good days and bad days. Then quickly changed the subject and asked me about my family.

I took a deep breath, the familiar sting of sadness and emptiness, not as strong, but still there before I answered. "I grew up in foster care."

Tegan's face showed genuine concern and empathy as she asked for more details. I explained that my parents were young and had just graduated from high school when my father was killed in a car accident. My mother struggled with his loss and was unable to care for me, so I was placed into foster care at the age of two.

"I'm sorry, Dayna," Tegan said softly, placing a comforting hand on my shoulder.

I shook my head and continued, telling her that I never found a permanent home or family through adoption.

"I remember being told by one foster family that I was sick as a young child, and that's why I wasn't adopted at an early age. Then another foster family told me, when I asked about my grandparents, that from what they understood, neither grandparent wanted anything to do with an illegitimate child as my mom and dad were not married. So, I was moved from foster home to foster home. However, during the last two years in foster care, I was placed with an older couple named the Browns, who were kind and supportive."

"Did you ever try to locate your mother?"

"I did. I tried in my late twenties. Then, when I was with Catherine, we attempted to locate her together. Unfortunately, we didn't have any luck."

As we drove toward hole seventeen, I added, "I was never mistreated. But it wasn't until I was with Catherine and our group of friends that I began to understand the meaning of family."

"Well," Tegan laughed, "when you meet my family, hang on to your hat because they will show you what it means to be family."

We arrived at hole seventeen, a short par three, and Frieda went first. Her ball landed on the far left of the green. Nedra's was on the far right. I took my shot, and it landed on the front edge of the green and rolled up four feet to the right of the hole.

"Nice shot," Nedra said from her cart. "Why can't I do that?"

I stood by our cart, facing Tegan, who was lining up her shot, then lowered her head. "Okay, Tegan, get inside me."

Tegan's club tumbled to the ground with a thud. Her eyes widened as she stared at me, her mouth opened in surprise. Behind me, Nedra and Frieda exploded into snickers, struggling to contain their giggles.

I turned to them. "What?" I turned back to Tegan, whose mouth was still agape. Her face was three shades of red. "What?" I asked again.

"Did you hear what you said?" Frieda asked.

"Yeah, I said for Tegan to get inside of...me...oh, shit." I covered my face.

Nedra and Frieda continued to laugh as I turned to Tegan. She covered her mouth, trying to hold back her laughter.

"Tegan. I meant for your shot, not—uh—you—your shot, your ball, to get inside my shot."

Tegan removed her hand, and her laughter blended in with the others.

I spun around to the others. "I meant for her shot to be inside mine, you know, between my ball and the flagstick." I turned back to Tegan. "*That's* what I meant."

Tegan collected herself, set up again, and took her shot. We followed the arch of her shot, and the ball landed just inside mine.

We all looked at each other and laughed.

Tegan winked. "I know what you meant."

I sank into my seat, and they all erupted in laughter again. I groaned, looking at everyone. "Oh, they'll never let me live this down."

Tegan smiled, leaned toward me, and said sweetly, "Yeah, probably not." Then added, "And I won't either."

CHAPTER TWENTY-EIGHT

As we drove back to my house, Nedra read off the scores. "Frieda had a hundred and two."

"That's the best I've shot. I can't wait to tell Cindy."

Nedra continued, "I had a ninety-four, my usual. Dayna had an eighty-nine, and Tegan had a ninety."

Tegan turned to the back seat. "That's definitely the best I've ever shot," she said, winking. "And it's all because Dayna put her hands on my hips and directed them into the correct position."

I heard a chuckle from the back seat as Tegan turned and smiled at me.

I wiggled my fingers on the steering wheel. "It's all in the hands."

"Well, your hands did the job."

"Hey, Dayna—anything happen after the golf outing with Scott and his family?" Frieda asked.

"Yeah. It's nothing, really. Denise, Scott's daughter, contacted me. She wants me to call her."

Nedra said, "Yeah, right. The Wolfords always want something." I heard a slap. "Ouch!"

I looked in the rearview mirror, and Frieda was staring at Nedra with a look that could kill. "The children had nothing to do with Vonda's choices." Nedra rubbed her arm.

"What are you going to do?" Frieda asked.

I shrugged. "Not sure. I'm still mulling it over in my head."

Tegan asked, "Do you know what she wants?"

"No. You know I recently saw them at the golf outing but besides that I haven't seen or heard from them for almost thirteen or fourteen years." I shrugged. "So, I have no clue."

"You need to give it some thought. You and Catherine adored those children, and they adored you," Frieda said.

I nodded as I turned down the road to my house. As I pulled into the driveway, Frieda said, "The weather was great, and the company was wonderful. Thanks for golfing with me."

"Anytime, Frieda," I said as we exited the car.

Everyone gathered their clubs and put them in their cars as I carried mine to the front porch. "Anyone want to stay for a snack or a drink?"

Nedra asked, "What time is it?"

Frieda looked at her watch. "Almost three."

"I'd love to, but I have a brief to research."

"I have to get home, too. I have to do laundry, mow the yard, and clean the house before Cindy gets home tomorrow," Frieda added.

"Okay." I looked at Tegan hopefully. "Tegan?"

Tegan looked between Nedra and Frieda, who had giant smiles, and then back to me. "Sure, why not? My brother is here this weekend with my mom. Just let me call him to tell him I'll be home a bit later."

"Great."

Tegan loaded her clubs into her car before pulling her phone from her back pocket.

As Frieda and Nedra backed out of the driveway, Frieda blew her horn and waved. Nedra followed, holding a hand out the window, and wiggled her fingers.

"Nedra, Nedra, Nedra."

Tegan bumped my shoulder. "She's a hoot. Is she always so sexual with her comments?"

"She's, uh, Nedra. We met playing club field hockey when we were in our midthirties. She can be obnoxious, but she'll stand by you, come hell or high water." I grabbed my clubs. "Let's go in."

Tegan stopped a few feet into the great room. "I like the openness."

"Yeah, that's why I picked this layout. Let me take my clubs to the garage. I'll be back in a minute. Make yourself at home. If you want something to drink, check the refrigerator."

When I returned, Tegan was standing in the dining room, holding a glass of water and looking out the window. Sunlight brightened her face.

"Hungry?" I asked.

Tegan stepped toward me and placed her hand on my cheek. "Yes." Her touch was soft, and our eyes locked. "I am."

I didn't move a muscle, and absorbed the warmth of her hand. I leaned into it. "Uh—I—" Tegan stroked my cheek with her thumb. I closed my eyes. "I could make hamburgers on the grill." My heart beat faster. "And I think I have the makings for a salad."

Tegan dropped her hand and stepped back. "That sounds fine with me. What can I do to help?"

My mouth dropped in disappointment. "What just happened?"

Tegan rushed through the door to the patio and took a deep breath.

I settled behind her. "Tegan?"

She placed her hands on the railing. "Dayna, I'm sorry."

"Sorry for what?"

She turned and leaned against the railing. "I'm attracted to you."

"Yeah, I noticed." I leaned against the railing, too, mimicking her stance. "And if you haven't noticed, I'm attracted to you too."

"So, what are we gonna do about this?" She moved off the railing. "This attraction?"

My heart raced as she stepped between my legs. I lowered my head and swallowed hard.

Tegan took another step and locked my wrists on the railing with her hands. Our bodies were inches apart.

My heart beat faster, and my breath shivered as I inhaled. Finally, I lifted my eyes, and I stared into pure desire.

"I—I—"

Tegan released my wrists and stumbled backward. "I'm sorry," she said as she raced back into the house. I followed Tegan and found her standing with the refrigerator door open. "I can make the salad."

I walked to her and closed the door. "Tegan. You're sorry about what?"

She gestured to the patio. "I don't know what came over me out there. I can't stop thinking about you." She swallowed hard and looked away, her face burning. She hesitated for a moment before meeting my gaze. Her eyes seemed filled with longing. "It's like electricity is buzzing between us when we're together. I want to touch you whenever I'm near you." Tegan walked into the great room and threw her arms to her side. "Well, fuck." She turned to me. "It's been so long since I felt such a strong attraction for someone."

My heart raced as I moved closer and felt her warm breath on my lips. With a gentle touch, I moved a strand of hair away from her face and traced the outline of her jaw with my fingertips. I marveled at her skin's softness and the allure of her full lips. Our lips met, and something coursed through my body as our mouths danced together. A deep moan escaped me as Tegan's hands moved to my chest.

Tegan suddenly broke away, gasping for air. "We've got to slow down," she whispered, her cheeks flushed.

My stomach twisted in knots. "Why?"

Tegan's eyes darted to the floor before meeting my eyes. "We need to talk."

I took two steps back, trying to steady myself. "Okay, how about over hamburgers?"

A small smile tugged at Tegan's lips. "And salad?"

I turned and opened the refrigerator.

CHAPTER TWENTY-NINE

I stepped through the patio door and onto the tiled surface surrounding the stainless-steel Weber grill, its lid glinting in the sunlight. The aroma of chargrilled burgers filled the air as I moved to the edge of the porch, overlooking the rolling fields. The sun behind my neighbor's slowly turning windmill created a kaleidoscope of color.

My stomach twisted with anticipation every time I saw Tegan, and my heart raced when she spoke. I wanted to be near her and gently touch her arm as we talked. A warmth flooded through me that I hadn't felt since Catherine. My gaze followed her as she weaved between the deck chairs and placed the salad bowls on the table.

When I caught her eye, she paused before me, brushing her hair away from her face. "Anything else I can do?"

My throat tightened. "Yeah, the ketchup, mustard, relish, and salad dressing should be in the fridge door."

Her eyes twinkled. She gave me a small smile and turned back inside. Moments later, she emerged with a selection of condiments and placed them carefully on the table.

"Thank you. That should be it. Just waiting for the hamburgers."

Tegan sat and watched as I returned to grilling. "Thanks for inviting me for dinner."

"Well, it's not much. But..."

A chair scraped across the patio, and then Tegan was beside me. "But?"

"You know, living alone. It's nice to share a meal with someone occasionally."

"If those hamburgers taste as good as they look, you can invite me anytime."

I grabbed the plate resting on the side of the grill and flipped the burgers onto it. "Let's eat." We walked to the table. I lowered a hamburger onto Tegan's bun and then one on mine. "Dig in." I grabbed the ketchup, squirted a circle on my hamburger, and reached for the relish. I looked at Tegan. "What do you need?"

"I need..." She drilled her eyes into mine. My stomach tightened as she pointed toward the condiments, her eyes never leaving mine. "I need the mustard and the Italian dressing, please."

I passed her the mustard and dressing, one in each hand.

"Thank you." She broke our connection as she squirted the mustard on her hamburger. She lifted the burger to her mouth. "This burger smells delicious." She took a bite, and the juices ran down her chin.

I grabbed a napkin, reached across the table, and wiped her chin. Her eyes never left mine as she chewed, and her shoulders wriggled in delight. She moaned as if she hadn't eaten in days. The sound shot through me like an aphrodisiac, thick, heavy, and ready to drop me to my knees. When she finished, she smiled. "Now *that* is a tasty burger."

I released my breath. "I'm glad you like it." I stabbed my salad. "You wanted to talk?"

Tegan sipped her Diet Coke. "On the railing, I locked your wrists so you couldn't move."

"Yeah?"

"I'm sorry for doing that."

I tilted my head, confused. "Why?"

"Because I can be assertive sometimes." She raised her eyebrows and smiled. "And I don't want to overstep any boundaries with you."

I hoped the sunburn from golfing covered my blushing. I cleared my throat. "I appreciate your honesty. But if you must know, it excited me when you did that."

Tegan's eyes widened. "Oh, really?" She took a deep breath. "Well, I didn't want to stop when you kissed me."

"Then why did you?"

Tegan stood up from the table and gazed over the open field. "My last relationship, let's just say I learned a lot about myself sexually."

I moved next to her. "What did you learn?"

"I sometimes like to be in control, and sometimes I don't."

"And that's a bad thing? I'm not understanding."

Tegan turned and leaned on the railing. "We started so fast and didn't talk much about what we like and don't like."

"Wait, what are you talking about?" I stepped away from the railing and stared at Tegan. "Are you talking about stuff that Cindy talks about as a KAP? Is that why you said what you said about pleasure?"

"See?" Tegan clenched both her hands. "It's freaking you out."

I stepped toward her and grabbed her hand. "No, it's not. It just surprises me. A kinky teacher?"

She smiled. "Oh, a teacher can't have kinky desires?"

I dropped her hand. "No. Yes. I don't know."

Tegan took my hand back. "The most important thing I learned from my last relationship is the power of communication and respecting each other's boundaries when it comes to having sex."

I jumped back. "Well, Catherine and I had started...I guess... experimenting."

Tegan smiled. "Sounds like you have some experience with kink."

"Well, I'm not sure." I inhaled and exhaled, then stood tall.

Tegan moved toward me. "Oh, you're wondering if you'd like to continue experimenting?"

I moved to the railing as Tegan approached me. "Yeah, maybe."

Tegan stopped. "Dayna, it's okay to ask questions. It's okay to talk about what gives you pleasure."

I walked to the other end of the patio.

Tegan followed. "Why do you keep moving away from me?"

"Because every time you get near me, my body goes crazy. The sparks fly everywhere."

"And..."

"And I haven't felt this way about a woman since Catherine." I walked to the table and collapsed into a chair. "And, if I'm being honest, the feeling is more intense."

Tegan followed. "That's why I said we need to talk. There's so much going through my head and heart right now with you being so close." She touched my shoulder. "I felt attracted to you the first time we ran into each other in the store."

"You mean when I ran into your cart?"

She smiled. "Yes. And I don't know the full story of you and Catherine, but I know from Stacy and Marilyn that it was a strong and loving relationship."

"I miss her." I looked into those hazel eyes. "But I know she would want me to move on."

Tegan ran her hand over my cheek. "Go on. I'm listening."

"I'd like to..." My heart pounded like a bass drum. Those eyes made my head spin. "I'd like to see where our attraction can lead us."

Tegan raised her other hand to my other cheek. "I'd like that too."

Her head dipped, and our lips met. A soft and gentle kiss sent a message of tenderness and caring.

When we broke our kiss, Tegan looked at her watch. "I need to go."

I widened my eyes. "That kiss sent butterflies to my toes. Is something wrong?"

"No. Absolutely not." She kissed me again and sighed. "I enjoy kissing you, and I felt the butterflies too. But I need to get back home to relieve my brother. He's already stayed longer than usual. Let me help you clean up, and then I'll head out."

"No, that's not necessary." I guided her through the patio door into the dining room. "You need to go. I'll take care of it."

"Are you sure?"

"Yeah." I waved my hands. "No problem." I walked her to the front door. "Thank you for staying."

Tegan looked into my eyes. "I enjoyed myself today. Can I see you again?"

I leaned my forehead against hers. "I'd like that."

She kissed my cheek. "Do you want to come to dinner at my house on Tuesday night?"

"I'd love to, but I leave Monday afternoon for Cleveland for a conference on Tuesday."

"When will you be back?"

"I haven't decided yet. My presentations are on Tuesday, so I thought I'd stay over Tuesday night and visit the Rock & Roll Hall of Fame before coming home on Wednesday."

Tegan's shoulders slumped. "How about Friday?"

A wide grin spread across my face. "I think that will work."

She stepped onto the front porch. "Call me when you get back from Cleveland, and we'll confirm the time."

"I will."

Tegan touched my hand and squeezed it. "Good night, Dayna."

"Good night, Tegan."

I returned to the house and collected the dirty dishes. I liked her. Besides the out-of-control attraction, I liked her. She was intriguing. I stopped in front of the dishwasher. Kink. Was that what Catherine and I were having? Kinky sex?

I watched the sun setting on the horizon, throwing orange, red, and yellow light over the open field. Tonight, Tegan's kiss had made me feel alive, and her abrupt departure left me wanting more.

A text vibrated my phone.

Thanks again for a beautiful evening.

You're welcome. Sleep well.

Good night, Dayna. See you when you return.

CHAPTER THIRTY

The conference room was packed, including the late stragglers standing in the back. Throughout my presentation, everyone focused on me and asked questions, reflecting their eagerness to learn.

I continued, "And you"—I pointed to the audience—"can do it, too, by believing in yourself, being your authentic self, and incorporating what you've learned into your leadership journey."

As the audience clapped, I scanned the room briefly. Then the moderator said, "That's all we have time for today. Please fill out your evaluation forms and drop them off on the table as you leave." She turned to me. "And thanks to Dayna Baldwin for being here today."

The crowd mingled and started to leave.

A woman with shoulder-length brown hair approached me. "Ms. Baldwin?"

"Yes?"

She was about an inch taller than me, dressed in black slacks and a white, silver-buttoned blouse under a pink blazer. Her many gold bracelets jingled as she extended her hand. "I enjoyed your presentation. It was motivating. I think I can conquer the world right now."

I shook her hand. "Thank you. Hold on to the energy and go conquer the world." When I pulled my hand away, she released it reluctantly.

"I'd like to learn more about your coaching services. A friend who attended another of your presentations told me you give personal, one-on-one"—she moved closer—"*hands-on* instructions."

I closed my eyes. Tegan's face flashed before my eyes.

The woman asked, "Are you okay?"

My eyes opened. "Yes, I'm fine. However, I have a luncheon date." I pulled out my silver business-card holder. "Here's my card. Give me a call, and we can discuss my services."

The woman looked puzzled. "But I heard—"

"I believe you heard wrong. Please excuse me. I need to freshen up before I go to lunch."

Heading toward the elevators, I stopped in the large lobby with cream-colored chairs dotted in pairs among white pillars. Tall, floor-to-ceiling windows faced the street, showing people hustling in every direction. I overheard someone talking about the weather and another about the new art exhibit downtown.

I spotted two unoccupied chairs with a small, round, glass-topped table between them. I threw my brown leather satchel on the table and flopped into a chair. I rested my head in my hands, wondering how I got into this predicament. The chatter and footsteps of people mingling in the lobby faded as my mind wandered.

First, I was angry after Catherine died, angry at everyone, disappointed in people and their lack of compassion. I'd lost all belief that there was goodness in people and was depressed about being unable to say goodbye to Catherine. Then, I restructured my routine and adapted to not being part of a couple. I'd told everyone I was fine yet my abandonment issues had returned in full force. I'd compartmentalized my life—especially my relationship life. But now there was Tegan.

"Dayna?"

I sat up and saw a familiar face. I blinked. "Denise." I shot up. "What are you doing here?"

She smirked. "I'm attending the conference."

"Really?"

"Yeah, I attended your presentation. I've been looking for you."

"Why?"

Her smile was now a frown. "You haven't answered my calls."

Denise was tall like her aunt, with eyes the shape of Catherine's. Denise had Catherine's strawberry-blond hair only shorter.

"I'm sorry I haven't returned your calls. I was planning to call you when I returned from this conference. So, I'm glad you're here. Please"—I pointed toward a chair—"join me."

"By the way"—she cleared her throat—"your presentation was awesome. I want to learn more about your five-step formula." Denise's leg bounced, and she twirled the conference bag strap on her lap.

"Thanks. So, why are you attending this conference?"

"I'm at the University of Dayton, studying for my Master's degree in Organizational Development with a nonprofit and community leadership certificate."

"That's great."

"One of our professors told us about this conference, and since it was in Cleveland, I could stay at home and only pay the registration fee. And then when I read the program, I saw you were a presenter, and I thought I could, um—"

I smiled. "Corner me and get me to talk to you?"

Denise shrugged and grinned. "Well. Something like that."

"Okay." I looked at my watch. "What are you doing for lunch?"

"Um, nothing. I was going to hang out here and get something from the hotel cafe."

"Well, how about we go to lunch and talk?"

Denise rose. "Sure. How about an Irish pub? Flannery's is close, and they have good fish and chips."

"Sounds good." I gathered my satchel. "Lead the way."

We walked out of the hotel's revolving door and approached the crosswalk. The orange hand was up, counting down five, four, three, two, and one. We stopped surrounded by at least ten people of different sizes and races, dressed in business suits and dresses, jeans and sweatshirts. Some talked on their phones, and others texted. Finally, the hand disappeared, and we all moved like a herd of cattle and crossed the street.

"Here it is."

We walked into the restaurant, and the hostess sat us at a table for two by the front window. We both ordered a soda and fish and chips.

I stared at Denise. "You look so much like Catherine."

"That's what my dad says." She ran her fingers through her hair.

I was unsure how to start this conversation, so I cleared my throat. "How are your father and the rest of your family?"

"Dad's doing much better, and he and Mom are happier. And Andrew is Andrew. Still, my little brother is instigating trouble and not getting caught."

"Fun trouble like when he complained to Catherine that you and I didn't buy him ice cream when we went to the zoo."

"Right. And Catherine believed him and took him to get ice cream while we stayed home. And he got a second cone." She took a deep breath. "I am so sorry for how Vonda treated you."

I held up my hand. "Denise, stop. You do not need to apologize."

"But—"

"No buts. You were a child. You had nothing to do with Vonda and her decisions. You do not need to apologize."

Denise sighed. "But her decisions impacted Andrew and me and our relationship with you and Aunt Catherine."

I laid my hand on top of hers. "Yes, it did. And I am sorry for that."

We sat silently, looking out the window, and watched people walking by.

"So, tell me about pursuing your organizational development degree. Why that major?"

She told me she wanted to be like Catherine, a successful, independent businesswoman. She felt that like me, working in the nonprofit sector empowered people to be their best.

Our server placed our fish and chips in front of us, smiled, and said, "Enjoy," before walking away.

"Okay." I reached for a fry. "Tell me more about how you'll utilize your degree."

With excitement, Denise explained how she wanted to become a nonprofit CEO or have her own consultancy to assist companies in improving their organizational culture. I listened intently and thought how proud Catherine would be.

When we returned to the hotel, Denise asked, "I called you to see if you knew of any jobs in the Dayton area. I'm looking for something part-time."

"Why? Your family has enough money."

"Just because I'm a Wolford—"

I raised my hands. "Sorry."

"It's a legit question. We have the money, but Dad insists we earn our keep. Andrew and I worked during the summers and had chores around the house."

"Good to know."

"Vonda tried her best to convince Dad that his children didn't have to work and that we're Wolfords, blah, blah, blah." Denise waved a hand. "Vonda's meddling was a big reason Mom and Dad lived separately for almost five years."

"Well, I'll keep my ears open, and if I hear of anything, I'll contact you."

"Great. And I'm looking for a place to live. My housemates are doing their internships and moving out, so I must find somewhere new."

We walked into the hotel lobby and returned to the chairs where we had met. "Do you want to stay on campus? What are you looking for?"

"Something close to campus would be great, but not necessarily. I have a car."

"Okay. Again, I'll ask around."

"Thanks, Dayna." Denise looked at her watch. "Oh, shit." She covered her mouth. "Sorry. My next session begins in five minutes. I gotta go." She jumped out of the chair and then hesitated before embracing me. She whispered, "Thanks for lunch and for talking with me."

I hugged her and pulled her close. "You're welcome. Thanks for being persistent."

She smiled and turned toward the meeting rooms before stopping and sprinting back to me. "Can we talk some more? I want to show you something. Not now—later, when we meet again?"

I looked into her young face, filled with excitement and hope. "Sure."

She touched my arm. "Great. I'll talk with you later." She hustled away.

As I watched her disappear around a corner, a voice behind me said, "You look refreshed."

I turned, and the tall brunette from my morning presentation stood before me. Her brown eyes roamed up and down my body. My usual desire to take advantage of lustful opportunities where I was in control began to stir.

My phone buzzed with a text. "Please excuse me." I reached into my satchel and looked at the screen. It was Tegan.

Hi. I hope your presentation went well.

I looked at my phone and back up to the woman before me, then back to my phone.

I stuck my phone back in my satchel.

The woman touched my arm. "Want to get a drink?"

"I have another presentation this afternoon."

Her delicate fingers curled lightly around my bicep, grounding me as I fidgeted nervously.

"You'll be exhausted after a full day of presenting." Her voice was laced with genuine concern.

My mind raced, trying to think of an excuse for why I couldn't meet with her later, but my body betrayed me by nodding in agreement. "I'll see you here at six," I heard myself say, surprising even myself.

She smiled, and her brown eyes sparkled with anticipation. "I'll be here."

CHAPTER THIRTY-ONE

As I entered Room B and approached the podium in front of the rows of tables and chairs, my heart raced. A flash of golden blond hair caught my eye, and my thoughts drifted to Tegan—our conversation, our kiss. I shook off the memories as people started filing into the room.

As my five o'clock presentation wrapped up, I thanked the participants for attending and packed up my laptop and notes. I strode past the registration desk toward the lobby, my anticipation growing with every step. The bar was already buzzing with activity as I scanned the faces.

The woman was perched on the high-top chair with her brunette hair, creamy skin, and almond-shaped eyes—nothing like Tegan. She spotted me and waved.

I sat next to her.

"My name is Linda."

"Hello, Linda. I believe you know my name."

Linda dipped her head. "Yes, Dayna Baldwin of Baldwin Executive Coaching for Women."

A young man with a white shirt and black jeans walked over and placed coasters in front of us. "What will you have, ladies?"

"Maker's Mark, neat," Linda said.

"A Yuengling, please."

"Coming right up."

A couple walked behind us and took the two seats at the bar next to Linda. Linda glanced at them, swiveled on the barstool, and her knee jammed into my thigh. "So, Dayna, have you changed your mind about my early request?"

"Your drinks, ladies." He placed the bourbon before Linda and my beer before me and asked, "Any appetizers?"

"No thanks." I looked at Linda.

"No, thank you."

"Well, if you need anything, my name is Derrick." He shuffled off to the couple next to Linda.

I took a swig of my beer.

Linda asked again, "Did you change your mind about my earlier request?"

"Maybe." My mind and body kicked into autopilot. Linda placed her hand on my thigh. I removed her hand and repeated, "Maybe."

"What can I do to make your maybe a yes?" Linda slowly lifted her drink to her mouth, running her tongue over her lips before sipping.

"Just know, if you persuade me to say yes, whatever happens, it's just sex and nothing else."

Linda's eyes focused on my lips. "Just sex. I can handle that." She leaned in and kissed me.

I pulled back as my mind flashed to Tegan standing between my legs, holding my wrists on the railing.

With a look of surprise, Linda asked, "Did I do something wrong?"

"No, nothing." I chugged the rest of my beer. "Take me to your room now."

Linda jumped off the barstool, dug into her purse, and threw twenty bucks on the bar.

She led me to her room on the tenth floor, where she scanned her key on the lock. I followed her as she flicked on the hall light. A king-sized bed was to the right, and a big-screen TV sat on top of a chest of drawers to the left. The windows were straight ahead, with sheer curtains that scattered the setting sun as it fell behind tall buildings.

Linda draped her pink jacket over the back of a chair in the far-right corner of the room. She wrapped her arms around my neck and, with her brown eyes, begged me to touch her.

I ran my hands down her breasts and stopped at her hips. I pulled them into mine and then dropped my hands to her ass. Our lips crashed together, mouths open, tongues battling for control.

My body felt like a car, moving through the gears, unable to break out of the routine for fear of damaging the gearbox.

Linda tightened her arms around my neck so our breasts pressed together. I moved my leg between hers. She ground against my leg, my hands on her ass guiding her. She moaned into my ear, and her breathing increased.

When she dropped a hand onto my breast, I grabbed it. "No. You don't touch me." I placed her hand back around my neck.

Linda's hips ground against me. My hands kneading her buttocks, the rhythm of our bodies creating a primal dance. I felt Linda's grip tighten around my neck, and I pulled away from her embrace. Our eyes met.

"Linda, I—I can't do this anymore."

Linda flopped on the bed, lips swollen. "What do you mean you can't do this anymore?"

"Look, Linda. It's not that I can't. It's that I don't want to do this anymore." I stepped toward the door.

Linda stood. "Can I do anything to change your mind to stay?"

I shook my head. "No." I opened the door and turned back to Linda. "Thanks for the drink." I walked out into the hallway, and the door slammed behind me.

CHAPTER THIRTY-TWO

I paced in my room like a caged animal. Stopping at the window, I took in Cleveland's glittering cityscape. In contrast to Linda's kiss, which had left me feeling empty inside, I remembered Tegan's touch. My body hummed with tension as I sat on the edge of the bed and reread Tegan's text.

I checked the time—six thirty.

I took off my clothes one piece at a time, throwing them on the floor as I walked to the bathroom and turned on the hot water in the glass-enclosed shower. I waited until steam rose, then stepped in, hoping to relax my body and empty my mind.

The steam engulfed me. I placed my hands on the shower wall as the hot water hit my head and cascaded down my body like a waterfall. Memories of my therapy sessions drifted back. The sound of my therapist's voice was almost palpable as her words echoed like a mantra, "The consequences of abandonment issues can lead to avoidance of emotional intimacy and sabotaging relationships."

A hollow laugh escaped me as I pondered all my one-night stands since Catherine died. I rubbed my face vigorously, wishing that hot water would wash away my thoughts.

I left the hot, steamy bathroom, condensation dripping down the mirror and clouding it. I wrapped myself in the plush white hotel robe. As soon as I entered the bedroom, a cold wave of air hit me, and my skin prickled, and my hair stood on end. I cinched the belt of my robe around me tighter and grabbed my phone.

I scrolled through my contact list before settling on Tegan's name. Trembling, I pressed the Call button and held my phone to my ear in anticipation. Time slowed as the line began to ring, and I debated whether or not this was a good idea. Before I had time to conclude, her voice came over the line—low but familiar. "Hi, Dayna."

"Hi. I hope I'm not interrupting dinner with your mom."

"No, she's watching TV."

"Ah—I—"

"You okay?"

"I—"

"Tell me what you need?"

After a few seconds of silence, I whispered, "I need to hear your voice."

"I'm here. Anytime you need me."

I took a deep breath, exhaled, and felt my whole body relax.

CHAPTER THIRTY-THREE

The following morning, I headed south on Interstate 71 toward Columbus, and eventually Dayton, reflecting on my conversation with Tegan from the night before.

Tegan had spoken about her two younger brothers, Nathan and Phil. Nathan was married, had two teenage daughters and worked in a high school near Sidney as a teacher and coach. Phil was a child psychologist at a children's hospital in Cincinnati and was single.

The two-lane highway turned into four as cars zoomed by me, no matter my speed. To avoid getting lost in my thoughts again, I reminded myself to stay focused on driving as I maneuvered through traffic.

Finally through Columbus, I continued west on Interstate 70, and as the traffic thinned, my thoughts returned to Tegan's voice. I remembered how she spoke so calmly and gently about her dad's service in the National Guard and his trips worldwide. The passing cars seemed like a blur as my mind wandered to our kiss and how her arms felt around me. I recalled the teasing about getting inside me. A contentedness washed over me as I found myself smiling.

In my daydreams, I imagined her on top of me in bed, my hands tied to the headboard while she nibbled my neck. Suddenly, I felt the rapid bumping of my steering wheel as I headed onto the right shoulder. Cursing, I refocused and got back on track, passing the Springfield exit completely unaware, lost in thought on Tegan, our conversation, and my fantasies.

I needed to pay attention to my driving, so I hit the audio button on the console screen, and my playlist came through the speakers. I sang along to "Mamma Mia" by ABBA.

As I approached my driveway, I noticed Marilyn's car parked by my mailbox. She reached out the passenger window and pulled open the mailbox door. Marilyn saw me in her rearview mirror and waved. Frieda, in the back seat, turned and waved. I pointed toward my house.

We met behind the cars, and Stacy held an envelope. "Hey, glad to see you." She hugged me.

Marilyn said, "It's Frieda's day off and we're returning from a wedding-planning lunch and wanted to drop off our wedding invitation. We weren't sure if you would be back from Cleveland."

"Yeah, I decided to leave early."

"You must have left very early to get home by noon," Stacy commented.

I opened my trunk and pulled out my overnight bag. "Not much to keep me there."

"Oh, no?" Frieda said with raised eyebrows.

I dropped my bag, spun on my heel and looked directly at Frieda. "What do you mean by that?"

"Whoa, Dayna," Marilyn said.

I leaned against the back of my car. "Sorry."

Frieda tilted her head. "Everything okay with you?"

Stacy rubbed my arm. "Yeah, anything happen in Cleveland?"

I picked up my bag again. "No, nothing happened. I'm fine. You want to come in for a while?"

Marilyn said, "No, we have to finish planning the ceremony with Frieda."

Stacy handed me the envelope. "This is the invitation."

I opened it, and it showed a picture of Marilyn and Stacy when they first met alongside a photo of them today. I embraced them. "I am so happy for you two."

Stacy said, "You know, Tegan is invited too." All three of them smiled.

Frieda added, "Maybe you two could come to the wedding together. I mean, Tegan did stay after golf last week. Anything you want to tell us?" She giggled.

Stacy smacked her arm. "Frieda!"

"What's going on?" I asked.

"Well, we're all thinking it, so I'll say it. I think you and Tegan would be a good couple," Frieda said.

I raised my hands. "Whoa! Where's that coming from?"

"Look, from watching you over the past few weeks, whenever you're around Tegan, you seem to—I don't know. You smile a lot when you're around her."

Marilyn said, "Frieda—"

"I know. I know." She flapped her hands in the air. "But, come on, Marilyn, don't you think it's time for Dayna to—"

I stared at her. "It's time to do what?"

"As in Ephesians, 'Let all bitterness, anger, and malice be removed from you. Be kind to one another, tenderhearted, forgiving one another.' I know the experience with Catherine's death and her family made you question the universe's core values of goodness."

"You got that right." I looked at Marilyn and Stacy and took Frieda's hand. "But since the golf outing and seeing Scott and his family, I don't know—it doesn't hurt as much anymore. When I saw Andrew and Denise, I realized life goes on, no matter what happens, and I need to try to move on."

"Oh, I'm so happy to hear that." Frieda squeezed my hand.

"Speaking of Scott and his family, guess who I had lunch with yesterday?"

"Who?"

"Denise Wolford."

"What?" Frieda's eyebrows rose.

"Yeah." I dropped Frieda's hand. "She was at the conference and attended my session. She found me sitting in the hotel lobby, we talked, and I invited her to lunch."

"Yeah, how did it go?" Stacy asked.

"We had a good talk." I informed them of our conversation and how she was looking for a part-time job in Dayton and a place to live.

Marilyn stared at me. "Didn't you tell me you're considering hiring someone to help you with your scheduling and billing a few weeks ago? And you do have an extra bedroom."

Stacy said, "Come on, guys. We gotta go." She kissed Marilyn. As they climbed into Marilyn's car, Stacy added, "Tegan did tell me she had a good time and that you cook a mean burger." She turned to high-five Frieda. Marilyn backed out of the driveway, blew her horn, and headed down the road.

I remained in the middle of my driveway, hands on my hips, and pondered. I did need help, and I did have an extra bedroom. I tilted my head back and forth.

I took my bag in and stepped onto the porch. I lifted my face to the sun, and its warmth engulfed me. Tegan told Stacy she had had a good time. My smile couldn't be contained as it stretched from ear to ear. Pulling my phone from my back pocket, I typed Tegan's name.

I'm home. What time on Friday?

Three dots in a bubble appeared on my phone.

I'm glad you're home safe. Dinner at six, but come early if you'd like.

I'd like. See you Friday.

See you Friday.

And thanks for last night.

Anytime.

CHAPTER THIRTY-FOUR

The next morning, I poured myself a glass of orange juice and strolled into my office. In the hallway mirror, I caught a glimpse of myself in my pale-blue blouse and comfy Gloria Vanderbilt jeans, and a faint smile found its way to my lips.

I sat in my Tempur-Pedic mesh chair and turned on my Apple iMac. I glanced at sticky notes along both sides of my monitor as I searched through piles of paper until I found my mouse. I removed a folder from the top of my keyboard and typed in my password. Finally, my schedule appeared for the rest of the week.

I scanned my calendar. "Damn it." I'd done it again—double-booked myself.

I wrote down Sarah Mitchell, a long-time client, and Donna Evans—who was that? Sarah and I were on a maintenance plan and met quarterly. I pulled her file and placed it on my desk. Now, Donna Evans—that name didn't ring a bell. I didn't find a folder for her under the E's in my file drawer and swiveled back to my desk.

I went through the three-inch stack of folders on my desk, and there it was, Donna Evans. I opened it and read my notes. Ah, yes, a new client from my last conference.

I called Sarah, and thankfully, she was willing to adjust her schedule so we could meet tomorrow. Then, a sticky red note on my monitor's bottom corner caught my eye. In capital letters was the word BILLING.

I searched and found my invoice-and-billing folder and rubbed the back of my neck. I was two months behind. I sat back in my chair. Well, the day was starting with a bang. I moved from behind my desk and surveyed my office. There was room for another desk.

I walked out of my office and down the hall into the second bedroom at the end of the hall. It had a full-sized bed to the right and a chest of drawers to the left. I rubbed my chin. There would be enough room in the corner for a chair and lamp.

As I walked back into my office, my phone rang with my publisher's ringtone. I reached back and felt my back pocket empty. I followed the sound to my desk and shuffled papers and found it under a stack of documents.

"Dayna, how are you?" Venessa asked.

"Doing well, how about you?"

"I'm peachy. I'm calling about the idea we discussed a few months ago about updating your book for a second edition. Have you given it some thought?"

"Umm...no. I haven't. I'm swamped with clients and conferences."

"Well, give it some thought, will you? Adding client testimonials and their stories would support your philosophy and approach to leadership."

"Okay, I'll think about it." I jotted it down on a sticky note—*Venessa and second edition*—and stuck it on the top corner of my monitor.

"Good, I'll call you in a few weeks. Ciao."

It was only nine thirty, but I felt like I'd been up for hours. I opened Donna's file and reviewed my notes to prepare for our ten o'clock appointment.

My stomach growled, and I glanced at the wall clock—six o'clock. I ached from sitting in the same position all day. As I wandered to the window, my eyes trailed over the carnage on my desk. I spun around to face my desk again, considering if Denise would be willing to help me. I did have a spare bedroom.

Walking through the dining room and into the kitchen, I stopped midway and remembered my dinner date with Tegan for tomorrow. Was it a date? Where did Tegan live? It was across from Meijer, but I didn't have her address.

I found a frozen pizza, put it in the oven, set the temperature and timer, and hit Start.

As I waited, I sat on my beige leather couch and called Tegan. Her phone rang two or three times, so I thought maybe she wasn't home. Finally, on the fourth ring, she answered. "Dayna?" She sounded out of breath.

"Tegan, everything okay?"

"Yeah, just finished dinner with Mom. She's not doing so well tonight."

I heard her mom in the background. "Tegan, how do I turn on this TV? I'm going to miss my show."

"Dayna, she's getting agitated. I need to go. I'll call you back."

"Don't worry, I just need your address. Text it to me when you have time."

Tegan yelled to her mom, "Just a minute, Mom, I'll be right there. That's right—about tomorrow. I've moved up dinner to an early dinner at four. Can you still make it?"

"Yeah, no problem. Look, take care of your mom. Just text your address."

"Thanks, I will. I can't wait to see you, Dayna."

My heart warmed. "Same here."

As I hung up, I heard Tegan. "Coming, Mom."

CHAPTER THIRTY-FIVE

After my rescheduled ten o'clock appointment on Friday morning, I jotted down notes in Sarah Mitchell's folder and filed them in the cabinet. My next appointment was at eleven thirty, so I took a break and wandered into the kitchen for a snack. My phone vibrated in my back pocket.

Morning Dayna. My address is 7501 Elin Court, off Hillgrove Ave.

Got it. Looking forward to spending time with you.

Mom will be with us.

No problem.

And...

And?

My brothers will be here too.

My thumbs froze.

Dayna, you there?

Yes. I'll be there, no worries.

Great. I'm looking forward to seeing you.

Me too. See you later.

Later xx

I stood in front of the mirror and surveyed my reflection. I was wearing medium-wash jeans that fit snugly around my hips and thighs and paired with a long-sleeved mock-neck sweater in a deep beetroot color. To complete the look, I chose comfortable black Cole Haan Chelsea boots. After one final check to ensure everything looked great, I grabbed my Eddie Bauer jacket as I headed toward the kitchen. The clock read three p.m. In her first text, she did say come early. So, I grabbed my car keys and walked out the door.

As I drove to Tegan's house, I thought about the what-ifs. What if her brothers didn't like me? What if I didn't like them? I liked Tegan, and that was what counted. That was what I needed to focus on—Tegan.

The house was a one-story, red-brick ranch with a two-car garage on the right. Tall pines lined the left side of the property. No cars were parked in the driveway, so I pulled to the garage door, leaving enough room for others to park behind me.

I walked by a bay window and saw Tegan's mom, Beti, sitting on the couch, watching TV. I could see the dining room table, and off to the left was a wide opening, probably to the kitchen.

I knocked on the front door. No answer. I knocked again.

When the door finally opened, Tegan stood wide-eyed and wiped her hands on a towel. "Dayna?"

"I know, I'm early."

Tegan brushed a strand of hair off her face. She looked adorable, dressed in blue jeans and a Toledo High School long-sleeved T-shirt, the cuffs frayed and a hole in one of the sleeves.

"Please come in. I didn't expect you to be early."

"Well, I was ready, so I thought I'd come over and see if you needed any help. Wow, what's that divine smell?"

"Lasagna."

"It smells delicious. Do you need any help?"

"Are the boys here?" Beti asked from the living room.

"No, Mom. It's Dayna." Tegan threw the towel over her shoulder and pulled me into the house. "Mom, this is Dayna. Dayna, my mother, Beti."

I reached out my hand. "Nice to meet you, Beti."

Her mom scooted closer to the edge of the couch and slowly staggered upward. She grabbed my forearm and stood. "We hug in this family," she said, embracing me.

I bent and circled my arms around her shoulders as she squeezed around my ribs.

She stepped away. "Do I know you? Are you Tegan's girlfriend?"

I looked at Tegan, smiled, and then back to Beti. "We met a few months ago at Meijer."

Beti flopped back onto the couch. "Well, I don't remember, but that's nothing new. So, are you Tegan's girlfriend? Because if you're the girlfriend who wasn't nice to Tegan, you can leave now."

Tegan sat next to her mom. "Mom, this is not Tiffany. This is Dayna."

Beti looked up at me. "Okay. Dayna. Let me tell you, you better be nice to Tegan, or you will have to answer to me."

I sat on her other side. "I promise you I will be nice to Tegan." I looked over the top of her head into Tegan's eyes. "I promise."

"Okay. So, do you play gin rummy? Her last girlfriend, whatever her name, didn't."

"Mom—"

I interrupted, "Yes, I do. Why don't you and I play while Tegan finishes cooking?"

"Tegan is cooking?" Beti nodded. "I remember. Nathan and Phil are coming for dinner. Right, Tegan?"

Tegan stood. "Yes, right, Mom. They should be here around four for your favorite—lasagna."

"Okay, so get the cards so Dayna and I can play."

Tegan closed her eyes, rubbed her forehead with her fingers, and deeply breathed.

I jumped up. "Where are the cards? I can get them."

Tegan smiled. "Thank you." She pointed to the hutch by the front door. "The cards are in the top drawer."

I opened the cabinet's top drawer and found a deck of cards among a few scattered coasters. I sat on the carpeted floor, facing Beti on the other side, and handed her the cards. "Your deal."

As we played our third hand, I asked Beti, "Is Betty short for Elizabeth?"

Beti waved her hand dismissively. "Oh, no, darling. It's a Welsh name. B-e-t-i, not B-e-t-t-y." Then she declared gin.

I shuffled and dealt. "Ah, I see. And Tegan is also a Welsh name?"

"Yes, it means 'beautiful and happy.'" Beti's gaze drifted to the dining room, where Tegan smiled as she set the table. "And she is truly beautiful."

"I heard that," Tegan chimed in.

"I couldn't agree more."

Tegan shook her head. "I heard that too."

"Gin!" Beti exclaimed triumphantly.

I turned back to her incredulously. "Not again." I tossed my cards onto the table. "That's four hands in a row. How do you do that?"

"Practice, my dear, practice."

"I think I need to stretch my legs for a minute. I'm not sure if I can even get up from this position." I grinned at her.

She laughed heartily. "Just wait until you're my age."

Tegan took a few steps and gave me her hand. I grabbed it and pulled myself up. I held Tegan's hand as we walked into the kitchen, where I pulled her close. "Can I help with anything?"

Tegan stepped closer and put her arm around my waist. Her eyes glowed, and her voice was gentle. "No. You're helping by keeping Mom busy. Thank you." She embraced me tightly, and I felt the warmth of her hug.

"My pleasure. I'm enjoying myself. She's telling me stories about her and your dad when they first married."

Tegan's eyes grew sad. "Yeah. She remembers those stories, but I'm not sure she'll remember you were here and played cards with her tomorrow."

I rubbed her back. "Doesn't matter. She's having fun now." I kissed her cheek and added, "The food smells delicious."

"It's Mom's favorite. Imagine a Welsh person loving Italian food. I need to start the bread since everyone will be here soon. Can you keep playing cards with her? It keeps her out of the kitchen."

I grabbed her hand and squeezed it. "Sure."

I returned to the living room. "Ready for another hand?" I sat back on the floor. "And this time, I'm winning."

Beti dealt the cards. "We'll see."

CHAPTER THIRTY-SIX

I shuffled the cards and dealt them to Beti when a loud argument at the front door caught my attention. Two teenage girls were bickering about who was driving to a football game while a middle-aged couple followed behind them, releasing exasperated sighs.

"Hi, Nathan and Liz!" Tegan called from the kitchen.

Beti furrowed her eyebrows and glanced at me, confused. "Who are they?"

My heart sank. "I think that's Nathan and his family." Beti stared blankly ahead for several silent moments before recognition filled her eyes. As if summoned by her realization, the younger girl walked up to us with a bright smile. "Grandma," she said as she took Beti's hand, "it's Madison, your favorite granddaughter."

A few seconds later, another girl grabbed Beti's other hand. "No, you're not. I am. Remember me, Grandma? Ashley, your other favorite granddaughter."

Beti regarded each granddaughter and smiled softly as if awoken from a dream. "Yes, you're both my favorites."

For what felt like an eternity, but it was probably less than a minute, we all stayed in that moment together. Beti was surrounded by her two granddaughters in a side hug, with joy radiating off their faces.

Ashley eventually broke the silence when she tilted her head and asked Beti who was playing cards with her. Before Tegan could answer for me, Beti said, "Tegan's girlfriend."

"Aunt Tegan has a girlfriend," said Madison. Her sister, Ashley, joined in on the cheer and wrapped their arms around Tegan while I sat silently watching their interaction.

Tegan wiggled out of their embrace, her face flushed, and her eyes darted around frantically. "No. Wait."

Tegan's face contorted into a glare when she looked at me, her hazel eyes narrowing. "Wipe that smirk off your face and help me here. Everyone, this is Dayna."

Without thinking, I reached around her waist and pulled Tegan closer to me in a hug. Her eyebrows shot up in surprise, then settled. At that moment, the front door opened, revealing another man Nathan quickly embraced in greeting. The girls joined them in a hug, calling out excitedly for their Uncle Phil while Liz smiled and looped an arm around my waist, telling me, "Dayna, welcome to the Roberts family."

Tegan took the opportunity to give me a gentle hug before walking back into the kitchen.

CHAPTER THIRTY-SEVEN

"Come and get it!" Tegan announced.

"It smells wonderful, Tegan," Liz said.

Madison and Ashley helped Beti off the couch. Madison said, "Come on, Grandma. Your favorite meal awaits you."

Beti and Ashley made their way to the dining room. Beti's shoulders were straight, her head held high. They stopped at the head of the table, and Beti gracefully took a seat as everyone else scrambled to find a chair. Liz shouted over the conversations, "Dayna, you can sit here." She pointed to a chair next to her. Tegan moved beside me, and I pulled out a chair for her.

The conversations stopped. All eyes were on me, and my neck grew warm. Finally, Tegan looked at me. "Thank you."

The chatter picked up where it left off. Phil loaded our plates with lasagna while Nathan passed the bread and salad.

"Mom, can I drive to the football game?" Madison asked.

"Mom," Ashley said, "I haven't driven to school all week because the car was being repaired."

Nathan looked at her. "Because you backed into a pole in the school parking lot."

"Well, I flunked the backing-up part of the driving test the first time," Ashley said.

"So." Madison sat straight as a board. "I should drive."

"We're picking up two friends, and Madison's only sixteen, so she can't drive with that many people in the car," Ashley said.

"Just because you turned eighteen, you think you can boss me around," Madison shot back.

Liz looked at both girls. "Okay. This is what we're going to do."

She looked at Nathan, who pointed back to Liz. "Whatever she says."

The girls slouched. "Okay. What's your plan?"

Liz explained that Madison would drive to pick up the first person, and Ashley would drive the remainder of the trip to the game. Then, on the way home, after Ashley dropped off the last friend, Madison would drive back to Grandma's house.

"Ugh, Mom," Madison whined.

Liz looked at Nathan and nodded as Tegan said, "Sounds like a good plan to me."

Beti asked, "Did someone feed Queenie?"

Phil gazed sadly at Tegan. "Mom," he said, his voice cracked. "I fed Queenie, and she's curled up in her bed in the living room."

"Okay, good. Can you pass me another piece of bread?"

As everyone chattered during dinner, Beti sat smiling, occasionally nodding her head. Her eyes flicked back and forth between each person as they spoke, some moments showing deep understanding while others revealing a hint of confusion.

Liz asked, "So, Tegan, now that you've met the Roberts family, what about your family?"

"Yeah," Madison said. "Does your family live around here?"

"Um." I hesitated. Everyone looked at me as silence reigned the room.

I let out a big, long sigh. Tegan turned to me and touched my shoulder.

My gaze met hers. "Well, I never had a family. I grew up in the foster care system." She tightened her grip on my shoulder, the warmth of her touch radiating through me.

When I glanced around at the table, I saw the look of shared understanding and sympathy etched on every face. "Catherine became my family when we were together."

Madison said, "I have a friend who grew up in foster care, and last year she got adopted. Did you have a chance to be adopted?"

"The foster care system was different in the late fifties and sixties. I was told not to get close to my foster parents because we didn't know how long we would be with a family."

"So," Ashley said, "what happened?"

"Ashley." Liz waved her hand. "Maybe Dayna doesn't want to share that with us."

"Well, okay. Sorry." She stared at her plate.

I looked at her. "Hey, Ashley." I winked. "It's okay. We're talking about families, so it's an okay question."

"So, what about your family?" Ashley asked again.

"Well, I probably stayed with ten or more foster families until I turned sixteen when I was placed with an older couple. By then, I had learned to rely on myself. But they helped me open a checking account, taught me how to drive, and helped me understand car insurance, among other things."

Phil added, "Sounds like you had to be on your own for most of your childhood."

"Yeah. The Browns, the older couple, didn't adopt me, but they were the closest I had to a family. They encouraged me to study hard and helped me apply to college. I played field hockey my last two years in high school, which helped me get financial assistance to go to college."

Madison asked, "Do you still see them?"

"No, they died a long time ago."

"I'm sorry," Liz said.

Madison jumped in and asked, "Who's Catherine?"

Beti asked, "Yeah, who is Catherine?"

Nathan waved his arms in the air. "Okay, let's give Dayna a break."

"No. I don't mind." I cleared my throat, and Tegan squeezed my shoulder again. "Catherine was my life partner. But unfortunately, she died in 2009 from a heart attack."

Beti looked at me. "I'm sorry, Dayna. I know what it's like to lose the one you love."

Nathan reached over and rubbed his mother's arm. "We miss him too."

I continued, "Catherine and I had a group of close friends who became my family, and through that family, I met Tegan." I reached up and put my hand on hers.

"We met at the charity golf outing, a fundraiser for the American Heart Association in Catherine's name," Tegan added.

Nathan and Phil jerked their heads in Tegan's direction. At the same time, they said, "You golf?"

Tegan smiled. "Yes, I do."

"Since when?" Phil asked.

"I took lessons last year, and I like it."

"Well," Nathan said, "we need to get together and golf. And next year, we can enter a team in the fundraiser."

Madison said, "I'd like to learn to golf."

Liz chuckled. "Yeah, let's add that to the twenty other things you want to do."

Tegan squeezed my thigh and kissed my cheek. Then she leaned back and grabbed the lasagna dish. "Who wants more lasagna?"

CHAPTER THIRTY-EIGHT

Throughout dinner, I shared how I'd met Marilyn and Stacy. Phil asked Tegan, "Stacy Bender, your best friend in high school?"

"Yeah. We reconnected once I came back to Ohio, and when I moved back here to live with Mom, we started hanging out again."

Beti said, "Stacy Bender?" She scrunched up her eyebrows. "I remember her. You two were inseparable."

Liz asked, "Is she married?"

"Well," Tegan said, "Marilyn and Stacy are getting married in two weeks after being together for nearly thirty years."

Ashley said, "That's great. Isn't it great that lesbians can get married now?"

Beti said, "Yes, it is. If I remember correctly, we both cried."

"Yes, we did." Tegan looked at me. "I believe every lesbian and gay man in the country cried that day. Anyway, it's time to clean up."

I said, "I'll clean up."

Beti said, "Who is she? And why is she going to clean up?"

I smiled at Beti. "I'm Dayna, a friend of Tegan's. She invited me to dinner."

Beti gazed at my place setting. "Well, she should clean up. Look at all those crumbs around her plate."

"She's worse than me, Grandma," Madison teased, pointing to her plate.

"Tegan invited you to dinner? Are you her girlfriend?" Beti asked.

I winked at her. "I'm working on it."

Beti giggled. "As long as you can play gin rummy, I approve."

"Everyone out of the kitchen," Liz said, ushering them away with broad, sweeping gestures. "Dayna and I will take care of the dishes. Tegan, you cooked, so you get a free pass."

The group shuffled into the living room and crashed onto the furniture. Liz rolled her sleeves and with a satisfied sigh, we eventually closed the dishwasher. Liz and I high-fived.

"Is it always this hectic?"

Liz nodded and smiled. "When we all get together? Yeah."

I smiled, too. "You're lucky."

I grabbed the faded blue dish towel hanging over the stove handle and dried my hands. Walking into the living room, I saw the girls sitting cross-legged on the carpet, playing Go Fish with Grandma. Nathan and Phil were intently focused on the football game. Tegan lay prone in the recliner, her mouth slightly agape.

I nudged Liz and pointed to Tegan. "She's asleep."

"Probably. Taking care of Beti is a full-time job. I don't know what we would have done without her moving back here."

One of Tegan's hands was under her head, her thick hair flaring over the headrest, and the other rested on her belly. Her breathing was slow and steady, and her chest rose and fell rhythmically. Her shoes lay discarded on the floor, one on each side of the chair. One knee was bent, and the other leg hung limply over the ottoman part of the chair. As I watched her sleep, my heart raced.

Madison and Ashley stood, thanked Grandma for a good game of Go Fish, and leaned in to kiss her cheek. Liz looked between them and reminded them about who was to drive and when. As they exited the house, their parents yelled, "Be safe and behave."

We settled back and watched the game.

"Did you see that?" Nathan yelled, standing.

"I know," Phil said.

"Come on," I said, "that was pass interference."

"It was not," Nathan retorted.

Tegan slowly opened her eyes. "What's all the yelling?"

She reached for the handle on the side of the chair and jerked it forward. The back of the chair popped up, and her feet went to the floor. Her eyes met mine.

"Your brothers are arguing about a call in the game we're watching."

"What time is it?" Tegan asked.

Liz said, "Nine thirty."

Tegan jumped up. "Mom!" She looked around. "Where's Mom?"

Phil put his arm around her shoulder. "She's in bed."

Nathan added, "Liz and I helped her to bed."

"Oh, sorry. I fell asleep. Thanks."

I asked, "You want something to drink?"

Tegan and I entered the kitchen and stopped in front of the refrigerator. I hugged her, and she wrapped her arms around my waist and rested her head on my shoulder. "This feels good," she said.

I lifted her chin with my finger, and as we stared into each other's eyes, we moved simultaneously until our lips met in a gentle, soft kiss. I broke the kiss but still held Tegan in my arms. "Thank you for inviting me. I enjoyed meeting your family."

Tegan kissed me again. "I'm glad you came."

Someone cleared their throat. "Okay, you two."

Tegan gave me a quick peck on the cheek and released me before turning. "Phil, you need something?"

"Not me, but maybe you do?"

Tegan charged toward him, and he dodged her. Nathan yelled from the living room, "What's going on in there?"

I yelled, "Sibling fight."

Liz and Nathan watched Tegan chase Phil around the dining room table, laughing. Finally, Phil stopped and opened his arms. Tegan ran into them, and they embraced. Phil said, "I love you, big sister."

"And I love you, little brother," Tegan said back.

Tegan's family was a picture of love and happiness, their arms slung over one another's shoulders in an embrace that showed deep affection. Curious about how such a strong bond had been forged, I asked how old they were.

Nathan replied that Tegan was the oldest at sixty-two, followed by himself at sixty, and the youngest being Phil, who was fifty-eight. They grinned as they all put their arms around each other's shoulders.

My voice caught when I commented on how wonderful it was that they maintained such a close relationship and had so much fun together.

Liz gave my arm a gentle squeeze. "It took me a while to get used to it, but now I couldn't be more thankful. And don't worry, there's always room for more."

Tegan broke out of the shoulder hold and hugged me. "Always room."

The TV announcer shouted, "Touchdown!"

We all turned as Nathan raised both arms over his head. "You've got to be kidding. Another one?"

CHAPTER THIRTY-NINE

We migrated back to the living room to continue watching the game. I plopped onto the couch, and Tegan nestled herself against my side, her head tucked neatly beneath my chin. I wrapped my arm around her shoulder, and she looked at me, her eyes sparkling in the dim light.

"I'm enjoying this," she said as I ran my fingers through her soft hair, and my body instinctively leaned toward hers. I smiled as our bodies connected in a familiar way.

"Me too." And my gaze returned to the TV.

"There are only eight minutes left in the game," Phil said. "It'll take a miracle for the Bengals to win."

"You better get out your wallet," Liz said.

We watched as the lead changed three more times. With three seconds left, Cleveland kicked a field goal to win.

Nathan jumped up. "Yeah! That's the game." He looked at Phil, held his hand, and wiggled his fingers. "You owe me twenty bucks."

Phil pulled out his wallet and handed Nathan a twenty.

Liz said, "The girls should be back soon."

I slapped my hands on my thighs and stood. "I should be heading home." I looked at Nathan, Phil, and Liz. "It's been great meeting all of you. Thanks for a wonderful evening."

Liz said, "Tegan, it's your weekend off from taking care of Beti." She glanced at Nathan. "Why don't you spend it with Dayna?"

"Liz!" Tegan's face started to turn red.

"Um." On a whim, I nodded and shrugged. "Fine with me. That would be lovely."

"Come on, sis," Nathan said. "It's our weekend here."

"Go have some fun," Phil said, wiggling his eyebrows.

The back of my neck heated up.

Tegan said, "Now, look, Phil, you're embarrassing Dayna."

Phil bumped my shoulder. "Go for it, Dayna."

I bumped him back. "I think Tegan needs a good night's sleep."

Liz said, "Probably, but she can do it at your place, where it'll be quieter than here." She moved toward the kitchen and added, "And I can send leftover lasagna home with you for lunch tomorrow."

"I'm sorry, but my family can be very pushy," Tegan whispered as she followed Liz into the kitchen.

I followed. "If you want to, I'm okay with it. I have a spare bedroom and no plans for the weekend." I wiggled my eyebrows. "It's up to you, but I'd really love to have you stay over."

Tegan took a deep breath and turned. "Okay. Let me pack a bag. It won't take me long." She left the kitchen and headed down the bedroom hallway, and Liz turned and smiled at me.

Phil and Nathan pumped their hands in the air. Phil cheered, "You go, girl."

I laughed as the girls burst through the front door.

Tegan reappeared with a brown overnight bag, saw the girls, and asked, "Who won?"

"We did," Ashley responded.

Madison looked at the bag. "Where are you going?"

Ashley punched her arm. "Where do you think?"

Madison covered her mouth and giggled. "Oh yeah. Girlfriend."

My face was growing warmer every second. "I—we—"

Liz laughed. "Dayna, stop. You don't need to explain anything."

As she walked to the closet, Tegan said, "Come on, Dayna." She grabbed our jackets. "Let's get out of here."

I turned and faced the group standing between us and the front door. I smiled at everyone, taking in their warm faces lined up next to each other. "Thanks again. I had a wonderful time."

Liz returned from the kitchen carrying a sizable Tupperware container. She handed it to Tegan and said in her kind voice, "Now, you two get out of here." We made our way along the line of friendly faces and paused briefly for hugs from everyone before we opened the front door. Liz called out after us, "Have fun."

I placed Tegan's bag on the back seat, and she put the Tupperware container on the other side. We both jumped into the car and sighed. I kissed her cheek, then rested my forehead on hers. "You okay with this?"

"Yes. I am."

"Okay." I backed out of the driveway.

CHAPTER FORTY

The night sky lit up with an orange-yellow glow from the streetlights, and as a few cars passed, their headlights briefly illuminated us both. Tegan's hand moved to my thigh. She paused momentarily before quietly saying, "So, you growing up in foster care, is that why you decided to focus on helping runaway and homeless children?"

"Yeah, like I said, the foster care system was different back then." I quickly glanced toward Tegan and put my hand on hers. "No one mistreated me, and I always had food and clothing." I thought back to earlier this evening. "But I never had what I saw tonight with your family—the fun, the teasing, supporting each other, the love you have for each other. The shared history..."

"What about friends? I bet it was hard to make friends."

"It was, but I started to once I got to college. My professors also believed in me and my ability to become a good counselor. I guess that's what got me to trust and believe in the intrinsic goodness of people."

Tegan squeezed my hand. "You seem to have turned out all right."

I turned onto the road that led to my house and continued, "The Browns helped me get into college, but what I didn't mention was that the most important thing they helped me understand was that people come into your life, sometimes for a short period and sometimes for a longer period, to help us on our life's journey."

"They sound like good people."

"The two years in their home were the best two years of my life up until then. Their kindness and generosity made me believe in people. My heart warms when I think of them."

"Did you stay in touch with them?"

I turned into my driveway. "Yes, until they both died. I was in my late twenties." The motion light above the garage turned on as I parked.

Tegan got out and looked around. "It's dark in the country." As I retrieved Tegan's bag from the back seat, she collected the lasagna container and added, "Quiet too."

"That's why I like it here. Only me and the solitude."

Tegan looked at me over the car roof. "Do you like living alone?"

"Uh, I like my alone time." I smiled. "But I miss having someone beside me in my solitude."

"Oh, I see." Tegan closed the door behind me and followed me toward the house. When we stopped, I pointed toward the sky. "Look up." The night sky was strewn with stars that stretched endlessly.

A collective gasp of admiration echoed between us. "Wow." She spun in a circle. "Look at all those stars!"

I grabbed her hand and guided her up the porch and into the house. "That's another reason I like living in the country."

I hung our coats in the closet and entered the great room.

Tegan turned. "I love your stone fireplace. I can picture you on the sectional before a roaring fire enjoying your solitude."

"Been there, done that." My stomach fluttered as I pictured us side by side on the sofa, doing more than sitting.

Tegan turned and dropped onto the sofa. "This is so comfortable. I could fall asleep right here." She covered a yawn with her hand.

"You look tired."

"It's been one hell of a week. First, Mom had doctor appointments almost every day. Then we had to go to the grocery store—a lot. Then, I had to get the house clean for the family. And finally, cooking." She patted the couch, and I joined her. "I'm glad you came early and kept Mom busy."

"I enjoyed it. She's a damn good gin rummy player. I only won one or two hands."

Tegan's eyes met mine, and her lips moved closer. Our mouths barely touched. But when I felt the warmth of her breath and the softness of her lips, I kissed her with a little more pressure. With each passing second, our kiss deepened with passion and intensity, creating a spark that ignited every nerve in my body, craving more of her. When Tegan gently pulled away, we shared a knowing glance that we were both entranced by what just happened. Tegan covered her mouth and yawned. "Dayna."

"Tegan." I placed my hands on her cheeks. "You've had a long week. You need to get some sleep." I stood and reached out my hand. "Come on, I'll show you to the bedroom."

Tegan slowly stood up and raised her eyebrows. "Your bedroom?"

"You're incorrigible."

"Okay." She grabbed my hand. "Show me the way."

I pointed to the left. "My bedroom is over there with an ensuite bathroom. And"—I pointed straight ahead—"you can use this bathroom." Then, I pointed down the hall to the right and started walking. "And your bedroom is through this door."

She touched the bedcover. "I like the green and the white trees on the duvet cover."

I placed her bag on the bed. "There's toothpaste and towels in the bathroom. If you need anything, please come and get me."

Tegan blinked her eyes, trying to keep them open. She stepped toward me. "You're right. I need a good night's sleep. If I did follow my"—she pulled my hips to hers—"desires, I'm afraid I'd fall asleep right in the middle of kissing you."

I kissed her forehead. "We have tomorrow."

Tegan backed away. "Thank you. I'll hold you to that."

"Good night, Tegan."

"Good night, Dayna."

CHAPTER FORTY-ONE

The following morning, I looked out the dining room window as the bright sun broke through the morning haze. Sipping my coffee, I contemplated the last few months and how rejuvenated and whole I felt. Denise needed a job and a place to stay, and I needed an assistant and had an extra bedroom. I had rejected an offer of a one-night stand. Tegan's family was accepting, kind, and fun. Marilyn and Stacy's wedding was the following week. I hadn't felt this hopeful since Catherine's death.

"Good morning," Tegan said.

I stared into her beautiful eyes and bright smile. She wore baby-blue pajamas, and her hair flew in every direction.

I cleared my throat. "Good morning."

Tegan ran her hands through her hair. "I must look a mess. I fell asleep when my head hit the pillow, and I don't think I moved all night. I bet my hair looks like a peacock's tail."

"Well, it's more like Christopher Lloyd from *Back to the Future*." I covered my mouth as a giggle escaped.

"Oh, so I look that funny?"

I placed the mug on the dining table and strolled toward her. I stroked my thumbs lightly down her arms until our hands intertwined. "No," I said softly. "You look beautiful." I lifted her hands to my lips and kissed them.

"Thank you." She covered her mouth. "I haven't brushed my teeth yet. But I would like a hug."

My arms surrounded her as her arms wrapped around my waist.

"Mmm," Tegan said softly.

We stood there for a few minutes, then turned toward the dining room window, my arm on her shoulder and her arm around my waist, and watched the sun rise into the blue September sky.

"Coffee?"

"Yes, please, with cream."

I squeezed her shoulder. "Coming right up. What do you want for breakfast? I can make bacon and eggs, or I have Special K." I handed Tegan her cup of coffee and the half-and-half next to it. "I don't know how much you use."

"Thanks. My mom says I have coffee with my cream." Tegan drowned her coffee to almost white.

I looked into her cup and laughed. "I think she has a point."

I sat next to her on the couch as we both faced the window.

"When I came into the room, you appeared to be deep in thought. What were you thinking about?"

"You. Catherine's niece, Denise." I bumped her shoulder. "You. Marilyn and Stacy's upcoming wedding. And you."

Tegan took a sip of her coffee. "This is Highlander Grog, isn't it?"

"Yes, my favorite." I took a sip, puzzled by Tegan's alacrity in changing the subject.

"Mine too. I hoped my sense of smell wasn't lying when I walked into the room."

I grinned. "So, what would you like for breakfast?"

"Coffee and toast will work for me this morning. I'm still full from last night's lasagna." Tegan patted her stomach.

I mimicked her. "Me too. I'll put in the toast and be right back."

When I returned with the plate of toast, Tegan was standing in front of the fireplace, holding a framed picture. She turned, smiled, and carried the picture to the table. "I'm assuming this is you and Catherine?"

"Yeah. Nedra took that. It was taken the summer she died." My heart warmed as moments of being with Catherine flooded my mind.

"She was gorgeous."

I nodded. "In so many ways."

"I'm sorry. I don't mean to—"

"Oh, please, you don't need to apologize. Catherine and I had fifteen wonderful exciting years together. Cut short, yes. But I'm so thankful for the time we had."

"I know Marilyn and Catherine were business partners, and Stacy told me about Catherine's heart attack. And I assume something happened between Catherine's family and you from the interactions with her brother at the golf outing?"

"Yes, it did."

"If you don't want to tell me, that's fine."

"No, it's fine." I started with Vonda disowning Catherine and rejecting her from the family real estate business, and then Scott finally coming around and meeting us for dinner. It ended with Catherine's heart attack and the horrendous aftermath with her family.

"You're kidding me. Her mother didn't allow you or your friends to visit or attend the funeral? She took all of Catherine's belongings." Tegan grabbed my hand. "How cruel. Dayna, I am so sorry. I can't imagine the heartache."

"It was devastating." I lowered my eyes. "I'd built my faith in people when the Browns showed me what it meant to be cared for. Then, when Catherine's family disowned her because we were a couple, my trust in the goodness of people wavered." I took a deep breath and released it. "We had our friends, and they became our family."

Tegan rested her hand on my arm.

"Then the drama after her death brought back my continuing issues of not being good enough, avoiding emotional intimacy, depression and anxiety, blah, blah, blah. My family stood by me, and, to this day, I don't know what I would do without them."

With gentle affection, Tegan stroked my face. I gazed at our coffee cups and tried to compose myself. "What do you say to one more cup?"

"Sure." Tegan smiled and collected my cup. Her fingertips grazed softly against the back of my hand. She leaned into me and kissed my cheek tenderly, and her lips whispered a quiet "Thank you."

CHAPTER FORTY-TWO

Tegan returned with our coffee, and we moved into the living room. On the sofa, Tegan tucked her feet underneath herself and rested against the arm. I sat at the other end and stretched my legs so my stockinged feet touched her shins.

"What would you like to do today? Or, I should ask, do you want to do anything today?"

Tegan reached down and rubbed my feet. "I have nothing in mind since this was a last-minute decision." She shook her head and huffed. "Or rather, it was a last-minute decision for *me* by my family."

I wiggled my toes. "I'm glad they decided." Then I wiggled my eyebrows. "It gives us time to get to know each other. Don't you think?"

"Stop that." Tegan slapped my foot.

"I must say, your family knows how to have fun."

Tegan smiled, a twinge of sadness in her eyes. "Yeah, I've been blessed with siblings who care for me and parents who love me." She lowered her head. "But I do miss my dad."

"When did you lose him?"

"About two years ago."

"I'm sorry."

Tegan hesitated. Her voice caught in her throat as she spoke. "He had liver cancer. He went pretty quickly once he got the diagnosis. We were all by his side when he left us—holding his hand, telling him stories, crying together. It was so hard to watch him fade away like that."

I moved to the dining room table, grabbed the picture of Catherine and me, and replaced it on the mantel. I traced my thumb along the glass and felt a lump forming in my throat as I whispered, "I wish I could have been by your side."

I felt warmth behind me as Tegan touched my shoulder. "I'm sorry. I didn't mean to make you sad." She wrapped her arms around me from behind and laced her fingers over my stomach.

I leaned back into her and placed my hands over hers. "I miss Catherine. Sometimes, I wonder what our lives would have been like now."

Tegan responded with a light kiss on my cheek and pulled me closer to her chest as if shielding me from further harm. Her steady heartbeat thumped against my back. Its rhythm brought me a sense of calm. Our shared embrace was filled with peace and understanding.

A phone rang, and Tegan said, "Not my ringtone."

It rang again, and I said, "But I like it here." The phone rang a third time. "I better answer it." I turned and gazed into her eyes. "Thank you."

I followed the ringtone to the couch. "Hello?" I covered the phone and mouthed to Tegan, "It's Denise."

Tegan returned to the couch.

"Sure. No worries. What time do you think you'll be by? Do you have my address?" I gave it to her and we said goodbye.

Tegan looked puzzled. "Denise? Scott's daughter?"

"Yes. She's attending UD and wants to stop by on her way back to campus tomorrow. Do you mind?"

Tegan smiled. "Am I going to be here tomorrow?"

I smiled back. "If you want to be. I would like that."

Tegan leaned her head on my shoulder and snuck her arm through mine. "Then I guess I'll stay."

We sat quietly until I asked, "Can I talk to you about Denise?"

Tegan sat up. "Sure. What's up?"

"I'm trying to control my...I'm not sure what. My excitement that maybe she wants to rekindle our relationship?" I told Tegan about Denise attending my presentation and lunch, my need to hire an assistant, and how Denise was looking for a part-time job and a place to live. "But—" I said, rubbing my face with my hands.

"But?"

"But what if she doesn't want this as much as I do?"

"Don't get ahead of yourself. She's coming tomorrow. Talk with her and see what she has to say. I'm assuming you had a previous relationship with her?"

"Yes. We spent time with her and Andrew. They came to visit us when they were younger until we informed Vonda that Catherine and I were a couple. Then all visits ceased."

"How old were they when the visits stopped?"

"I think Denise was in fifth grade, and Andrew was in third. So about ten and eight years old."

"Well, you must have left an impression if she wants to see you now."

"I guess I'll have to wait until tomorrow and find out."

Tegan jumped up. "Now, I need a shower."

CHAPTER FORTY-THREE

I watched Tegan walk away, her hips swaying rhythmically. I was tempted to follow, but carried our coffee cups and plates to the sink and let the moment's warmth linger. I headed to my bedroom, where I changed into jeans, a white T-shirt, and a striped L.L.Bean pullover.

As Tegan set foot into the living room, her dark jeans hugged her curves, and a fitted gray sweater showcased the strength of her toned stomach. Her movements exuded confidence and grace that drew me to her even more.

She tumbled onto the couch. "Oh, I feel so much better."

"Good." I continued our conversation. "So, you know about Catherine and me. Are there any serious relationships for you?"

"One. Her name was Tiffany." Tegan fidgeted with her hair.

I remembered Beti mentioning that name. "How long were you together?"

She twisted her body from side to side. "About four years."

"You seem reluctant to talk about her."

"She's why I hesitate to act on my attraction toward you." She was silent. "She and I—well, she—I—God, I practiced how I would explain this." Tegan smiled, reached for my hand, and spoke like a rapid-fire machine gun. "Tiffany liked to be in control."

I nodded. "Oh."

"Tiffany took the dominant role when we had sex."

"Okay."

Tegan paced the room. "Then one night, I used my safe word, and—" Tegan stopped before the fireplace and put her hands on the mantel. "And she didn't stop."

I stood and moved toward her.

"I've never told that to anyone before."

"Did she hurt you?"

"No, but she scared me." Tegan turned toward me. "She apologized, but I couldn't trust her sexually, and our relationship was never the same. We broke up, and I moved to Toledo."

"Have you been with anyone since?"

"No." Tegan stepped toward me. "But now that I've met you and am attracted to you"—she grabbed my hand—"strongly, I might add, I needed to talk to you about this before we go any further."

"So, you have experience with kink?"

"Well, if you're into BDSM, I guess so. But like I said at the pool, why must we label everything? Whatever gives a person pleasure, whether that's being tied up, oral sex, or whatever." Tegan rested her hand on my cheek. "You're blushing."

I laughed. "I know. I can feel my face turning red."

"So, what about you?"

"Me?" I stepped back. "Umm. Well." I glanced over Tegan's shoulder at the picture on the mantel. "A few months before Catherine died, we started to share our desires to be more sexually adventurous."

"Interesting. Continue."

"We started experimenting."

"Experimenting? How?"

The heat in my stomach moved up to my neck and face. "Using blindfolds and talking dirty and—"

Tegan moved closer and leaned her lips to my ear. "And what did you learn?"

"I learned—" My heart skipped a beat. "I learned that I like to be teased, and—"

Tegan stuck her tongue in my ear. I swallowed hard.

"And." My voice was barely audible. "I'm embarrassed to tell you."

Tegan moved away from my ear and turned my face toward her. "Dayna, you don't need to be embarrassed."

"Who thought at our age we'd be talking about kink?" I chuckled.

"Age is irrelevant." She leaned back to my ear. "Now tell me, what gets you wet?"

My clit jumped to attention, and I moaned. She wrapped her arms around my waist and pulled us together. Our bodies touched from our breasts to our thighs.

Tegan's voice was low and quiet, but its demand was unmistakable. Her eyes were fixed on mine as she spoke, and I felt that complying with her request was nonnegotiable. "Tell me, Dayna."

I held her gaze. My voice was slow and steady as I explained how I enjoyed slow teasing, punctuated by sharp bites of pleasure.

Tegan brushed her cheek against mine, moving her mouth toward my ear. "Like this?" She bit my earlobe.

My heart fluttered, and my stomach clenched. A high-pitched "Yes" escaped.

As her hand moved over my breast, I heard rapping.

"Is that a knock at the door?" She bit my neck.

"Uh—" All the muscles in my body tightened.

Three more loud knocks.

I moaned. "Yeah."

"Should we answer it?" Tegan whispered, then licked my ear.

My skin prickled and burned. My mind was shrouded in a thick fog. "Answer what?" I managed to croak, my parched lips barely moving.

"The door."

"Uh. No."

"Dayna?" Tap. Tap. "You home?"

"It's Stacy," Tegan said as she pulled away from me.

I reached for the mantel and exhaled as my legs buckled.

"You okay?"

"No." I grabbed her hand and put it over my heart. "Do you feel that?"

She raised her eyebrows. "Answer the door."

As I did so, I felt Tegan's breasts against my back and her hand squeezing my ass.

Stacy and Marilyn looked at us, then at each other, and then back at us. Grinning, Stacy said, "Geez, Dayna, you look flushed. Did we interrupt anything?"

Tegan lowered her chin onto my shoulder, and her arm surrounded my waist. "Nothing that can't be continued later."

I waved them both in, and Tegan, by my side, slipped her hand into the back pocket of my jeans.

Marilyn said, "We were just driving past and wanted to invite you to dinner, but now that you have company, would both of you like to join us for early dinner?"

I looked at Tegan, and she nodded. "Sure, we'd love to. We were just discussing what we were going to do today."

"Well, if you like to come around two, we could play euchre before dinner," Stacy suggested.

I squeezed my thighs together, and I thought. *Hell, yes, I want to come.*

Tegan squeezed my butt. "That sounds fun."

I asked if we could bring anything.

"No," Stacy said, "just you and your girlfriend?"

Tegan winked at Marilyn and Stacy. "We're working on it."

CHAPTER FORTY-FOUR

Tegan's mouth twisted into a frustrated grimace. "I keep forgetting the bar is also trump and the second-highest card in the deck."

We threw our cards in the center of the table as Marilyn wrote down the score. "That makes it eight to one," she said, her tone light but her expression tinged with pity.

"Don't rub it in," I grumbled as I collected and shuffled the cards.

"Speaking of Trump," Marilyn said, "as Frieda would say, God help the United States of America—and us—if he becomes the Republican nominee for president." My stomach rumbled noisily, interrupting Marilyn's political commentary. She cocked an eyebrow and looked at me. "Hungry?"

I put my hand on my stomach. "Sorry. But the smell of your pot roast is the culprit."

A wide smile spread across her face, and she stood from the table. "Then let's eat."

Stacy said, "Get what you want from the fridge."

I jumped out of my chair, headed to the fridge, and turned to Tegan. "What would you like?"

She walked and bent over me from behind, running her palm over my stomach, her fingertips inside the front of my jeans. "You." She nibbled my neck.

I groaned as chills ran down my spine.

"Um, some of us would like to get something to drink," Stacy said as she stood at the kitchen's entrance.

Marilyn added as she sat the Crock-Pot on the table, "Hey babe, can you get me a Diet Coke, please?"

"I'd love to, but Dayna's girlfriend is making her blush, and she can't find what she wants to drink."

I covered my face and leaned my head back onto Tegan's shoulder.

Marilyn looked into the kitchen and shook her head. "Stacy. You appear to be correct."

Tegan kissed my head. "What do you want, Stacy? I'll get the Diet Coke."

"Same, thanks."

Tegan moved around me, retrieved two Diet Cokes and a regular Coke, and then looked at me. "Dayna, what would you like?"

I reached around her and grabbed a Diet Sprite. I brazenly squeezed the soft curve of her backside and playfully dodged her outstretched arm as I quickly moved to join the others at the table.

"This is so delicious," I said as I finished my second helping of pot roast.

Marilyn pointed to my plate. "Look at those bread crumbs around your plate. How do you do that?"

I picked up my plate and shrugged. "I'm not sure."

"I noticed that last night at dinner," Tegan said.

Stacy looked at me. "You and Tegan had dinner?"

I looked at Tegan and back to Stacy. "Yes, I had dinner with her family. The lasagna was delicious. And yes, I had crumbs."

Marilyn chuckled. "Some things never change." We all laughed as I gathered and dropped my crumbs on my plate.

"Dayna, have you thought about the second edition of your book?"

Tegan tilted her head. "You wrote a book?"

"That's why she gets invited to present at conferences," Stacy said.

"Oooh, an author. I'm impressed."

"Don't be." I felt myself blushing.

"Come on, Dayna," Marilyn said. "You're helping women develop leadership skills, and God knows we need women leaders more than ever."

"Tell me more," Tegan said.

As we gathered dishes, I explained my book, its premise, and how it ignited my consulting business.

"When did you start your business?"

Stacy looked at me encouragingly.

"Um, I wrote the book a year before Catherine died, and when it was published, I started getting requests from women to help them. I realized that by three years without Catherine, I needed to make a change, so I sold the house—too many memories—and built a new home and started my consultancy."

"Yeah!" Stacy high-fived me. "And she's been in demand ever since."

"Good for you. So will you do a second edition?" Tegan asked.

We moved into the living room. "I'm still thinking about it. I don't know how to do that timewise. I can barely manage my commitments now."

Marilyn sat next to Stacy and said, "You did mention you might be hiring someone to help you."

I placed my arm over the back of the couch and rested my hand on Tegan's shoulder. "Yeah, I need to think seriously about it all."

"So," Tegan said, looking over to Marilyn and Stacy. "Next Saturday is your wedding. Are you excited?"

Marilyn reached for Stacy's hand and stared into her eyes. "Yes, very."

Tegan said, "I'm excited for you too."

My gaze left her and drifted out to their backyard, where the sky had settled into a burnt orange hue with the sun slowly sinking behind the treetops.

"Excuse me," Tegan announced, heading to the guest bathroom.

Marilyn looked at me curiously as she knitted her eyebrows together. "What's wrong, Dayna?"

I met her gaze before looking away. "Catherine would be so happy for you."

Stacy nodded. "We miss her and know she'll be with us in spirit."

"Yes," I replied softly.

When Tegan returned, the corners of my mouth curled into a smile at the sight of her.

Marilyn reached across and grabbed my hand, sensing something unspoken between us. "And Catherine would be happy for you too," she whispered.

CHAPTER FORTY-FIVE

As we walked into my house, I turned to Tegan, my eyes wide. "What were you trying to do to me back at Marilyn and Stacy's?"

Tegan backpedaled with a smirk. "What do you mean?"

My palms sweated as I approached her, my heart racing. I grasped her arms and pulled her close. The warmth of our bodies radiated against each other. My mouth was dry with anticipation. I looked into her eyes. "You know."

She retreated backward, cautiously measuring the space between us with each step until her legs bumped against the dining room table. I moved closer, watching her grab each chair and move around the table to create a barrier between us. A playful glint twinkled in her eyes as she smiled shyly. "You mean when I ran my hand over your stomach and reached into your jeans? And licked and bit your ear?"

"And when you stood behind me and pressed your breasts into my back." I growled like a lion and lunged toward her. She laughed and scrambled around the couch. My arms encircled her waist from behind and yanked her back to me as I spun us around. Our bodies pressed together, and we both gasped in pleasure. Never breaking eye contact, we turned together as she pushed me gently back onto the couch.

My body was like a time bomb ready to explode. I wanted Tegan to devour me with her hands, mouth, tongue, and teeth. I needed her skin against mine.

As if reading my mind, Tegan stepped back, and her breathing deepened. "What do you want, Dayna?" Her eyes seemed pierced with desire.

"Tegan," I began, eyes closed, the haunted memories and the hollow feeling when I left my one-night stands overwhelmed me. "Since Catherine died, I haven't been touched by anyone."

Tegan's body relaxed. "We can stop." She paused. "I will never do anything you don't want to do."

Taking a deep breath, I opened my eyes and met hers directly.

"Dayna, we can use red to stop, yellow to slow down, and green to keep going. You will always be in control."

I marched toward her, our bodies inches from each other. "I want—" I took a deep breath.

Tegan's eyes bored into mine. "Tell me."

"I need you to touch me. I want to feel your skin on mine."

Her face started to flush, and her breathing increased with mine.

"I want you to kiss every inch of my body and send me into oblivion."

I didn't know who moved first, but our lips mashed together, and our tongues battled back and forth like wrestlers, each trying to pin the other.

"Take me to your bedroom." Tegan jumped and wrapped her legs around my waist.

I stumbled.

"Whoa. Steady there."

"I'm not as strong as I used to be." We both laughed as Tegan slid down my body and stood.

"It looks so sexy in the movies." We both laughed again. "Okay. So, let's try this." Tegan took my hand, kissed it then my lips. "Lead me to your bed."

My heart pounded with each step.

We stood beside the bed, moonlight the only light in the room. Tegan moved her body to mine, leaned in, and bit my earlobe. "I want to see your face when I make you come."

My nipples came to attention, and I slowly reached down, never taking my eyes off her. I fumbled for the lamp. A soft hue cast over the top half of the bed.

"Perfect. Now turn around," she said in a low voice filled with anticipation. I turned to face the bed. "Take off your shirt."

Tegan's hand softly touched my arms as my shirt dropped to the floor. Her bite on my shoulder sent goose bumps over every inch of my body. She unhooked my bra, and her hands cupped my breasts gently. Tegan moaned into my ear. "I can't wait to suck them." Without warning, she dropped her hands, and the warmth of her body disappeared. I started to turn.

"No."

I stopped and leaned my hands onto the bed, and sighed deeply. I rubbed my legs together, trying to release the pressure between them.

"I want to show you what I was thinking when I was behind you in front of the refrigerator."

I glanced behind me and saw Tegan undressing and quickly turned away. Then I felt her breath on my neck, warm and inviting as her breasts pressed against my back. Her left hand meandered across my stomach and then grazed across the top of my pubic hairline, sending a thrill throughout me.

"You told me you like to be bitten." She touched my shoulder, and I heard the anticipation in her voice. "Can I bite your shoulder?"

Without hesitation, I panted, "Yes."

As Tegan's teeth grazed my skin, I arched my back and let out a low moan. "Harder," I gasped, gripping her hand on my breast. She obliged, increasing the pressure of her bite, sending waves of pleasure through me.

"You're killing me here," I growled, trying to catch my breath. Her hand slipped down my pants and underwear, teasing me with her fingers.

"You did say you like to be teased."

"Yes," I gasped, but she pulled her hands away and stepped back. My eyes widened as I took in her naked body, small breasts, soft curves, and a mischievous grin on her face.

"Do you like what you see?" She pointed to my remaining clothing. "Off. Now."

I ached with desire, my chest was heavy with longing, and my heart pounded in my ears. I was desperate for human contact. I stripped off the rest my clothes, and Tegan watched every move.

She pointed to the bed. "Lie on your back."

My body shook with excitement as I adjusted the pillow under my head.

"Remember our safe words?" she asked, crawling onto the bed. "Red means stop." She moved between my legs. "Yellow means pause." I spread my legs invitingly. She lifted my right leg and gently nibbled on the inside of my thigh. "And?"

"Green to continue."

She gently continued to nibble the inside of my thigh. "Color?"

"Green."

Her lips traced a path up my left leg, leaving a trail of nibbles that turned into bites. My body responded with shivers and throbbing between my legs. I gripped her shoulder, begging for more. "Tegan, please."

She leaned back, my leg draped over her shoulder, and wiggled her finger playfully. "Ah ah, no touching. Hold on to the headboard and keep your hands there, love."

I grasped the wooden slats as my leg fell back onto the bed.

Tegan continued to tease and tantalize me, kissing and biting her way from my navel to my breasts. She licked my hard nipple before gently biting down, sending waves of pleasure through my body. My hips started to rock uncontrollably as I struggled to catch my breath.

Tegan lifted her head, her breathing mirroring mine. "Want it harder?"

"Yes."

She complied, biting down harder and causing me to gasp, and my hips lifted off the bed in search of more.

"Is that too much?"

I shook my head, and, with a wicked grin, she moved to my ear and whispered, "Now the real fun begins."

CHAPTER FORTY-SIX

When I woke and looked out the bedroom window, the sun was halfway over the horizon. The dazzling rays of pink and orange reached into the blue sky. I turned under the blanket and maneuvered to spoon Tegan, sleeping on her side, and rubbed my hand over her curvy hip and ass.

A soft moan from Tegan reignited my desire. A quiet laugh escaped my lips as I planted soft kisses on her shoulder and let my fingernails glide down her spine. I gently pulled her closer, my hand resting lightly on her breast.

She pressed her hips into me, and her body moved against mine. Her voice was a soft growl. "You want to go another round?"

I squeezed her breast. "I could get used to waking up this way every morning."

Tegan covered my hand with hers. "Oh, you could, could you?"

I stopped, turned onto my back, and stared at the ceiling.

Tegan turned and rested her head on her elbow, her other hand on my stomach. "What's wrong? Your body just went stiff as a board."

I turned toward her and dropped my hand on top of hers. "Last night and early this morning was—I never—my body's reaction to your touch—I can't find the words." I took a deep breath. "As you've probably gathered, since Catherine, I've only had one-night stands, with me in total control." I kissed her palm. "And I don't want this to be a one-night stand. I want more of you. I want to spend more time with you."

"Dayna—"

"No, let me finish. The women I picked up would always ask me to stay the night. I never did. I was always up-front about no commitments, no strings." I brushed her hair behind her ear, resting my hand softly on her face. "But I don't want to leave you. I want to stay."

"Well, we *are* at your house, so you have to stay." Tegan snickered.

I frowned. "Tegan, I'm serious here."

Tegan smiled from ear to ear. "So, you want me to be your girlfriend?"

"Yes, I want you to be my girlfriend."

My mouth crashed against hers in a kiss that made my temperature skyrocket. When we parted, I panted, "I'm so glad you're here." I swallowed hard. "Now, want to take a shower?"

Tegan grabbed my hand and led me into the bathroom.

CHAPTER FORTY-SEVEN

We finished a pancake breakfast and sat on the couch to discuss Marilyn and Stacy's wedding, Hillary Clinton's pneumonia treatment, and the Obama administration's plans to increase the number of refugees admitted to the United States. All the while, some part of our bodies were touching. Tegan's hand on my thigh, my shoulder next to hers, and her leg over my lap made me believe nothing could come between us.

"So, I need to move and do something, or my muscles will be sore tomorrow," I said as I reached for Tegan's hand. "You gave me a workout last night and this morning."

Tegan kissed my nose. "Do I hear a complaint?"

I shook my head adamantly. "No, ma'am." I returned her nose kiss.

"There's a walking path just down the road. Remember we crossed it when we went to Marilyn and Stacy's. Do you want to go for a walk?"

"Yeah. That sounds good."

We scrambled off the couch, and as we headed out the front door, I stopped and hugged Tegan. "Ready?"

"Yeah, let's go."

My hand grabbed Tegan's, and we walked along a paved path surrounded by tall pines and dappled sunshine. The air was sweet with the scent of pine, and birdsong echoed around us. Tegan turned to me, her eyes twinkling in the early light. "This feels right."

"I'm a little nervous about meeting with Denise later this afternoon."

Tegan squeezed my hand. "Why?"

"From what I sensed during our talk in Cleveland, she has Catherine's drive and ambition."

"That's a good thing, right?" Tegan faced me. "Don't overthink it. Have an open mind." She placed her hand on my chest. "Keep an open heart and listen to what she has to say."

I covered her hand with mine. "Thanks. I can do that."

As we continued to walk, the trees disappeared, and cut-corn fields surrounded us. I lifted my face to the warm sun, and suddenly Tegan squeezed my hand and stopped. "Look." She pointed to her right. Standing in the field about fifty yards away was a herd of deer. All six heads popped up from grazing and stared at us as we stared back. "Aren't they beautiful?"

I moved behind her and wrapped my arms around her waist. "Beautiful like you."

"You know how to get to a girl's heart."

I placed my chin on her shoulder. "And I want your heart."

Tegan stirred something inside me that I thought had died with Catherine. For so long, I'd become emotionally unavailable.

Tegan turned in my arms. "Well, Ms. Baldwin." She rested her forearms on my shoulders. "I'm considering giving my heart to you. If you promise to cherish and take care of it."

As a lump formed in my throat, I wondered if I could make that promise. "I'm scared of trusting again." My voice cracked.

"Dayna." Tegan ran her hand over my cheek. "All I'm asking for is a chance to make you want to stay."

We turned to the herd of deer as they dropped their heads and started eating again. Hand in hand, we silently walked back toward the house.

Tegan called her brother and walked with her cell phone pressed to her ear, her forehead creased with worry. She spoke in low tones and paused, listening intently. Her eyes darted around the room as she spoke, pushing her hair from her face. Finally, she hung up and took a deep breath before turning to me. "Mom had another restless night around three o'clock, but Nathan said she's doing better this morning."

We sank into the couch together, and Tegan explained her increasing concern about her mother. Her brows knitted together as if deep in thought. "We need to do something about the wandering at night. I'm terrified she'll leave the house and get lost."

"Well, I'm sure there are support groups or agencies that can direct you to resources to help with those things."

"Yeah, I did some research and when I get back home today, we're going to FaceTime with Phil and begin the discussion."

I pulled her close and kissed the top of her head. "If there's anything I can do, please tell me."

Tegan wrapped her arm around my waist. "You're doing it."

We sat silently and drifted asleep until a knock at the door woke me.

I opened my eyes as Tegan stirred. "Is someone here?" I gazed at the time on my phone. "Uh, Denise is coming, but not for another hour."

I moved to the door, stretched my arms above my head, and glanced back at Tegan, who winked.

I opened the door, and there stood Denise, dressed in jeans and a red UD sweatshirt, holding a Nike shoebox. "Hi. I realize I'm early, but traffic wasn't as bad as I thought."

I opened the door wider and invited her in.

She stopped as Tegan walked toward her. Denise's eyes bounced back and forth between us. "Am I interrupting anything?"

"No. Are you Denise, Catherine's niece? I believe I saw you at the golf outing. I'm Tegan." She extended her hand. "Nice to meet you."

Denise shook it. "You were with Dayna's group of friends." Denise glanced back at me as she followed Tegan into the living room. Her eyes widened, and her head turned like an owl between Tegan and me. A wide smile appeared. "Gucci."

I turned to Tegan. "Gucci?"

Tegan and Denise chuckled. Then Tegan said, "It means cool. Good."

I smiled. "Gucci."

CHAPTER FORTY-EIGHT

"Would you like something to drink?" I asked.

"Sure, whatever you have will be fine," Denise answered.

My hand trembled as I grabbed a Diet Sprite from the refrigerator. Tegan and Denise talked animatedly, but my mind was preoccupied with the ominous shoebox on Denise's lap. With a tight smile, I handed her the soda, but her gaze kept drifting back to the box.

Denise slowly brought the can to her lips and took a sip. After a long pause, she presented the box like a gift and muttered, "I know I told you I needed help finding a part-time job, and I still do, but this is why I've come."

My heart raced as I gently placed the box on my lap.

An uncomfortable silence hung in the air until Denise finally spoke, her voice barely audible. "I don't know where to begin."

I ran my hand over the top of the box, trying to calm my nerves. "Do you want me to open it? Will that help?"

Denise nodded weakly. "Why not? Go for it."

I lifted the lid and looked up at her in confusion. "Cards? A shoebox of greeting cards?"

Her face contorted with sadness. "Yes. Cards." She grabbed one and read it to herself, her forehead creased. Slowly, she handed it to me.

I read and saw the familiar signatures. My eyes widened in shock, and my hand instinctively covered my mouth. Tears welled as Tegan rubbed my back reassuringly. I moved to another card, this time a Christmas one. It held the same names inside, and so did the next one. I turned to Denise in disbelief, tears streaming down my face. "You kept all of these cards that Catherine and I sent you?"

Tegan leaned in closer and smiled at Denise.

Denise stood and moved to sit beside me. "Yes, I kept every single one. Well, almost all of them. Vonda intercepted a few and told Andrew and me we simply wouldn't accept any more cards from you and Catherine. Dad was furious."

My voice caught in my throat as I stared at her. "You kept all of them? Even after everything that happened?"

Denise nodded solemnly, tears glistening in her eyes. "Yes, because they were from Catherine and you—our aunts we missed."

I picked out another as Denise continued, "Andrew kept his, too. He wanted to be here, but he's in Illinois at Northwestern studying business and has a big paper due. He would like to get together with you, too."

"Studying business."

"Yeah. He already has his realtor's license but wants to get a business degree as well. He wants to become a partner in the family business."

Catherine and I sent Hallmark cards for all the kids' birthdays and holidays, and postcards with goofy messages during other times of the year, even after Catherine was kicked out of the family. We shared stories about our lives, hoping that someday we'd get a response. But with every passing year, it seemed more and more unlikely.

"Yeah, see?" Denise grabbed a handful and put them on the couch between us. "This one is from when I was five years old." She handed it to me with a grin.

I shook my head in disbelief. "You got them *and* kept them." I embraced her. "Catherine would be so happy." I wiped my tears, and Denise wiped hers. "I've been hoping for this day for a long time."

Tegan hugged me. "I'm so happy for the two of you."

Denise continued recounting how her dad had intercepted the cards so Vonda wouldn't know about them and how she and Andrew looked forward to learning about our lives. Then she shared her memories of us playing games and swimming in the Wolford pool.

Finally, Tegan stood. "Sorry to interrupt, but I need to get home. Nathan and the family need to leave in about an hour."

I jumped up. "I'm sorry. I forgot the time."

Tegan smiled. "I am so happy for you." She pulled me close and hugged me hard. "So, so happy for you." When we pulled away, Tegan said, "Denise, it was good to meet you. I'll let you two continue to get reacquainted."

Denise stood and lifted her chin in the air. "I think Catherine would approve."

I grabbed Tegan's hand and looked at her. "So do I."

CHAPTER FORTY-NINE

On Friday night, I sat on my couch, diving into a pint of Turkey Hill chocolate ice cream, feeling like I had had no time to breathe. My week was bombarded with new clients, and I needed to catch up in sending out invoices. I had a conference in Seattle in a few weeks, and my publisher called last night about the book. I discussed with Denise the possibility of moving in and working for me part-time and was ecstatic when she told me she knew about computers, spreadsheets, and scheduling programs. I had my fingers crossed that it would all work out.

As I sucked the ice cream off my spoon, thoughts of my weekend with Tegan and her passionate bites made my body shiver... Or was it the ice cream? I took another bite and fantasized about Tegan standing before me naked, holding a blindfold and handcuffs.

Tegan's ringtone interrupted my fantasy. "Tegan." I cleared my throat. "I was just thinking about you."

"I was thinking about you and calling to confirm I'm still meeting you at your house tomorrow for the wedding at two. Right?"

"Yeah. Two. And I can't wait to see you."

"Me too."

"Oh, by the way, how's your mom?"

Tegan had discussed the next step for her mom's care with her brothers. They decided to get a home security system with cameras that record inside and outside the house. The system would be wireless, inexpensive, customized to their needs, and connected to all their phones so that they could monitor their mom from anywhere. They were also going to talk to the doctor about changing her medication.

"Good. I'm glad to hear you have a plan."

"Have you heard from Denise?"

"No, not yet. I'm hoping to hear from her this weekend."

"Look. I need to get going. I want to get a good night's sleep so I can enjoy the wedding festivities tomorrow and later with you," she said, her voice becoming low and husky.

CHAPTER FIFTY

On the morning of Marilyn and Stacy's wedding, the gang worked tirelessly to oversee the setup for the big day. The event company rolled out the heavy oak dance floor in the backyard, anchoring it securely to the ground. In anticipation of rain, they assembled a white canopy above the floor, ensuring it was sturdy enough to withstand any potential downpours.

Nedra and I carefully strung colorful Christmas lights along the edge of the shelter, adding a touch of whimsy to the otherwise elegant setup. As an added precaution for unpredictable weather, we strategically placed stainless-steel heaters, ensuring the guests would be comfortable no matter what Mother Nature had in store for the day.

Frieda wiped the tables as she rehearsed the First Corinthians verse she would recite during the ceremony. Cindy leaned in and whispered, "Throw in some kink terminology for fun." Frieda laughed and playfully tossed the towel she was using in Cindy's direction.

Nedra and Leslie were lovey-dovey as usual, sharing their plans for their December wedding.

When I left, about twenty chairs had been placed in front of the curved row of trees in the side yard, where the ceremony would occur. The backyard was ready for food and dancing, and I was ready to return home and shower.

Since my house was close to Marilyn and Stacy's, Frieda, Cindy, Nedra, and Leslie came with me to freshen up. As the four of them walked through the front door, holding small overnight bags, I told them, "You know where the bathrooms are. I have towels and washcloths on the beds for everyone."

Cindy said, "Hey, I heard you and Tegan are coming to the wedding as a couple."

Everyone stopped and slowly turned toward me.

"Did I hear my name?" Tegan asked as she stood at the front door, smiling widely.

She carried an overnight bag in one hand and an apricot blazer in the other. My heart raced. Her blue floral-print dress had a deep V neckline, revealing alluring cleavage.

Everyone turned to Tegan and then back to me. Cindy said, "Yes, you heard your name. I was asking Dayna if what I heard about you and her is true."

I approached Tegan and when I looked over my shoulder at our friends, felt my cheeks redden. I leaned in and, as I kissed her, her lips parted, and the tip of her tongue touched mine. She dropped her blazer and wrapped her arms around my waist, pulling me closer.

Everyone clapped when we parted. We rested our heads on each other's foreheads and laughed. Then I turned to them. "Does that answer your question, Cindy?"

Frieda gave us a giant hug. "Oh, my prayers have been answered. I'm so happy for you both."

Nedra slapped me on the back. "It's about time."

Tegan placed her head on my shoulder and hugged my waist.

I flapped my hands and silenced everyone away. "Okay, we better get ready for the wedding. We can't be late."

I picked up Tegan's belongings and followed Nedra and Leslie into my bedroom. I threw Tegan's blazer and bag onto my bed. "Don't take too long in here. I need to get ready, too."

Cindy and Frieda headed down to the guest bedroom. I grabbed Tegan's hand and led her to the patio. My phone rang while we stood there enjoying the sun, the birds singing, and the breeze.

"Hey, Denise." After a few minutes, I covered my phone and whispered to Tegan, "She said yes!" Denise and I planned for her to move in the following week and start working with me as soon as possible.

I hung up and leaned against the patio railing, staring at the sky. "Who would have thought? Catherine and I always hoped to resurrect our relationship with Andrew and Denise."

Tegan stepped between my legs. "Well, it's happening, and I'm so happy for you. And I'm sure Catherine is looking down with a smile."

I nodded and pulled Tegan close. "Thank you for understanding and accepting my relationship with Catherine."

"Well, Denise did say it was gucci that we're together."

I smiled. "I think it's cool too." I grabbed her hand and returned to the house. "Why don't you come to the bedroom in a few minutes after I shower and help me get dressed?"

As we passed Nedra and Leslie leaving the bedroom, Tegan said, "You two look comfy and bright." Leslie was in floral, wide-legged pants and a yellow, short-sleeved blouse, and she carried a black shawl. Nedra wore a bright red blouse tucked into low-riding jeans, black suspenders, matching red sneakers, and a jean jacket.

"I don't know how anyone will beat your outfit, Tegan," Nedra replied.

I wrapped her in my arms. "She's all mine."

As I changed my clothes, Tegan's eyes were on me every second. "Please stop."

"I don't know why you're putting on underwear because it will be ripped off later tonight." She took a step closer. I ran my tongue over my dry lips as my heart and clit began to pound.

"Ripped off your body with"—her face was so near, she leaned and bit my neck and licked my ear—"my teeth."

As Tegan advanced toward me, I swallowed hard and stumbled a few steps back until I fell onto the bed. I jumped up and extended both arms. "You need to back away, or I will have to change my underwear."

Tegan smirked, walked backward through the door, and pointed at me. "You did tell me you like to be teased."

I squeezed my legs together and pointed. "Out. Now."

Her chuckle floated back into the room as she left.

When I joined the group in the living room, the air was vibrating with conversation. Everyone was engaged in the circle of animated discussion, gesturing and nodding as murmurs of laughter and debate swirled around them. I clapped my hands, and everyone turned. Tegan gave me the once-over in my dressy jeans, white button-down blouse, lightweight brown leather jacket, and black Doc Martens boots. She turned back to the group. "She's mine."

CHAPTER FIFTY-ONE

After the ceremony, the guests moved to the backyard, where the caterer had set out appetizers of bacon-wrapped dates, butternut-squash and apple bruschetta, and deviled eggs. Shrimp, potato and leek soup shooters, a vegetable tray, flattened roast chicken on a board, and salmon with homemade hollandaise. Of course, there was a chocolate cake for dessert. The outside bar was stocked with beer, wine, and hard liquor.

Marilyn's and Stacy's parents, all in their mideighties, sat at a table with Rebecca and some of Stacy's teacher friends.

We sat and chatted about the ceremony. "Didn't my wonderful partner do a great job as the officiant?" Cindy asked.

Frieda leaned into Cindy and blushed. "You're biased."

Tegan pulled me close. "I thought the way they incorporated the scripture reading about love said it all."

I watched her as the group continued their discussion and remembered the scripture: *Love is patient, and love is kind.* When I touched Tegan's arm, she glanced my way, smiled, and returned to the group. *Love always protects, always trusts, always hopes, always perseveres.*

My eyes focused on Tegan and how her face lit up when interacting with our friends. Her expression was warm and genuine, and her cheeks flushed slightly when she laughed. She spoke with her hands, emphasizing points and guiding conversations. She met my gaze every few minutes to check that I was still here. I was in awe of this woman who had touched my life and given me hope for a happier future.

The sound of someone tapping a glass drew our attention to the married couple's table as they kissed, and then we all clapped.

The sun started to descend, and the lights on the canopy came on. Marilyn and Stacy made their way to the dance floor for their first dance as a married couple to the Indigo Girls' "Power of Two."

We surrounded the edge of the dance floor. The newlyweds' gazes were joined, their bodies moving rhythmically, their love radiating. We swayed to the music until Marilyn waved her arms for others to join them. Cindy and Frieda were first, with Nedra and Leslie right behind them. Other couples joined as Tegan nudged me. "What are you thinking?"

"Uh...nothing."

"Yes, you are." She stood in front of me. "Tell me."

I exhaled. "Just thinking about how wonderful Marilyn's and Stacy's families' support for their relationship has been over the years."

Tegan touched my cheek. "I'm sorry you didn't have that."

"Oh, don't get me wrong. I'm thankful for everyone here who I call my family." I pulled her close. "And I'm most thankful for you coming into my life." I tilted my head back. "God, I think Frieda is wearing off on me."

Tegan chuckled, grabbed my hand, and pulled me onto the dance floor as a slow song began. We wrapped our arms around each other. "And I'm thankful Stacy invited me to the golf outing, and you jumped my dead battery." She laughed, then bit my earlobe and neck, knowing what it did to me.

I growled. "Later." And spun her in a circle.

We swayed in time to the song, and our bodies melded as one. I savored the feeling of her breath on my neck, and my hands traced languid circles down her back. Her fingertips grazed my scalp, sending sparks through me.

Over the next couple of hours, the guests gradually left, leaving our family of eight dancing and laughing on the dance floor. The next song was "We Are Family" by Sister Sledge, and we formed a circle with Marilyn and Stacy in the middle, arms raised, swaying, and singing along to the music.

The music faded away. Marilyn's eyes shone in the Christmas lights on the canopy as she moved into Stacy's embrace. She glanced back at us over her shoulder, her face illuminated by the soft glow in the darkness. "Thank you all for your friendship and love over the years and for celebrating this wonderful day with us. You all enrich our lives so much."

"Oh, stop," Frieda said with tears in her eyes.

Leslie stepped forward. "I continue to be in awe of your bond with each other and the longevity of your friendships. I am so happy to be part of it. So, thank you for accepting me into your group."

Tegan cleared her throat and held my hand. "I second that, Leslie. I cannot thank Stacy enough for reconnecting with me and introducing me to all of you."

Cindy added, "You both fit right in, girlfriends."

I shot out my hand. "Wait a minute." I pointed at Tegan. "She's *my* girlfriend."

Frieda lifted her arms to the sky. "Thank you, Jesus." At which everyone laughed uproariously.

On the short ride back to my house, Tegan rubbed my thigh, nibbling my ear and neck.

"Stop."

"Hurry." She stuck her tongue in my ear.

My whole body shivered. I stopped suddenly, realizing I had driven past my driveway. Tegan chuckled as I put the car in reverse and pulled in. As we raced through the house to the bedroom, my mind went wild about what I wanted to do with Tegan.

I entered the bedroom behind her and Tegan pushed me against the wall. She stood facing me, her eyes full of lust, and stepped toward me. I stepped back and hit the door. As she pressed her body into mine, I grabbed both her hands and, in a quick move, held them above her head and spun her. I plastered my body against hers against the door. The heat of her body competed with mine as I stared at her demanding lips and then at her flaming eyes.

My lips crashed against hers as her breasts and hips slammed against mine. I held her hands tightly against the door and used my foot to spread her legs. I stepped between them and slammed my thigh into her crotch. Her heart pounded against my chest as she moaned.

"Dayna," Tegan panted my name. "Dayna."

I dove in and licked her neck to her ear. "Tonight, I'm in charge."

I stepped back, our bodies no longer touching, still holding her hands above her head, and waited for Tegan's answer.

She licked her lips. "Green."

CHAPTER FIFTY-TWO

The following weeks flew by as Denise settled in. We discussed her school schedule and created a to-do list, including finding a scheduling program, composing a letter introducing her as my administrative assistant, searching for client-management software, and booking flights and hotels for my upcoming conferences.

Andrew, Denise, and I spent a day together when he had a break from Northwestern. We reminisced about our times together and his hopes for the future. Seeing how he had grown into a caring and ambitious young man was wonderful.

I called my publisher and told her I'd do the second edition of my book. Denise would contact former clients to gather testimonies, allowing me to focus on work.

I arrived in Seattle for the conference, and Tegan's absence was heavy in my heart. Every night, I'd picked up the phone to hear her reassuring voice and ask for news on Beti. Her mom was getting more forgetful at night but the video cameras were helping ease their worry.

One night a week, Tegan and I planned a dinner or lunch with Beti either out or at my house, depending on her lucidity. It was good to see the glint in Beti's eyes when she chatted about old memories, and she didn't let me forget how many gin rummy games she had won.

Whenever Tegan's family was in town Friday night for the weekend to take care of Beti, we played board games and laughed before we returned to my place for the remainder of the weekend. We often met the gang for a night out or laughed around the fire pit in my backyard, or Tegan and I sat on the couch, me quietly reading a book and Tegan reviewing Denise's school papers, always touching, holding hands, or cuddling.

I'd built so many walls because I feared loving again and having that love taken away from me. But Tegan and her family led me back to believing people are kind, decent and generally honest. The Robertses considered me part of their family, and along with our family of friends, I was happy and hopeful.

My heart swelled with love whenever I gazed into Tegan's eyes. Our skin seemed to melt together, and every caress was electric with emotion. We shared a deep, unspoken connection while making love, though neither had said it out loud.

One day, after lunch at my house with Beti, I began thinking about Thanksgiving. "Why don't we celebrate Thanksgiving here?"

"You mean, with all of my family?" Tegan asked.

"Sure. Why not?"

I watched Beti sitting on the couch with Denise as she explained why I was going to Pittsburgh the next week.

Tegan whispered, "You serious?" When I nodded, she looked at her mom. "Excuse me, Mom?"

Beti turned to her. "Yes?"

"What do you think of having Thanksgiving here at Dayna's this year?"

Beti's eyes roamed my house, and she nodded. "Your place can hold all of us?"

I smiled. "I think so." I gazed around the room. "We'll make it work."

Beti's eyes opened wide, and she glanced back and forth between Tegan and me. "You cook?"

"Well, not exactly."

"You've never cooked a turkey?" Beti asked.

"Ummm...no."

"Well, how are you going to cook Thanksgiving dinner?"

"Yeah? That's a good point," Denise chimed in.

I sat down next to Beti. "Well, I'll have it catered."

All three turned toward me and responded in unison, "What?"

"Why not?" I jumped up and cleared my throat.

Denise said, "What's up, Dayna?"

I took a deep breath and sat back down next to Beti. "Beti." I grabbed her hands and squeezed them to ensure she was focused on me before I continued, "Beti, your family has taught me what it feels like to be part of one." Tegan moved and sat next to her mom. "I was never part of a family. And I want to do something for all of you to show how much I appreciate you. That's all. I want to do something for you and your family."

Tegan turned to her mom. "What do you think, Mom?"

The silence was deafening as she thought it over.

Finally, Beti raised her hands to my cheeks. "Having Thanksgiving with you in your home will be wonderful. Now give me a hug."

I embraced her as I glanced at Tegan and Denise. Both exhaled a huge sigh of relief and smiled.

CHAPTER FIFTY-THREE

Thanksgiving morning, Denise and I ran around the house frantically cleaning, arranging furniture, and adding chairs to accommodate nine for dinner and four more for Marilyn, Stacy, Cindy, and Frieda, who would bring pumpkin pie and ice cream for dessert.

A deep-red, orange, and burgundy bouquet sat in a plum-colored glass vase in the middle of the dinner table. Two rustic bouquets of sunflowers, bicolor roses, and orange-and-rust chrysanthemums were at each end of the fireplace mantel. Between them were pictures of Tegan and me around the fire pit, Tegan's family eating lasagna, and our family of friends at Marilyn and Stacy's wedding. There was one of Denise, Andrew, and me sitting at the table playing a board game, and another of Catherine and me rounded out the display.

I stepped back, and my heart warmed. I now understood what Frieda meant when she said I was blessed.

I set the table using white china framed by fine silverware from my foster mom, Mrs. Brown. I stepped back, put my hands on my hips, and observed our efforts throughout the room.

Denise mimicked my move, then nodded and crossed her arms over her chest. "Looks good."

"You're sure your parents are okay with you spending Thanksgiving with me?"

"Yes, for the umpteenth time. I'll be with them for two weeks during Christmas break. Or I should say, you'll be free of me for two weeks."

"I enjoy you being here." I wrapped my arm around her shoulder and smiled. "And, of course, being my assistant." I wiped my brow, then gazed at the stove clock. "Okay, I think we're ready."

After I showered, I returned to the living room, and the doorbell chimed. A glance at my watch confirmed it was one o'clock. The caterers brought the preroasted turkey, mashed potatoes, sweet potatoes, green beans, sweet-and-savory stuffing, cranberry sauce, and rolls. They set the food on the counter, left the instructions, with me staring at containers lined next to each other like a train.

I looked at Denise. "This can't be hard. We follow the instructions. Right?"

With a quick nod, Denise agreed, "Right."

I rubbed my hands together. "I can do this."

Denise walked around the counter and inhaled. "Everything smells delicious. I can't wait to taste it all."

I wanted this day to be full of good food and laughter. *Just follow the instructions*, I told myself. My heart stopped for a beat as I spun in a circle. "What about drinks?"

"Calm down. Remember, Tegan and her family are bringing them."

We both collapsed onto the couch and high-fived each other. "We did it."

We agreed to meet at two o'clock, and right on time, there was a knock at the door. The whole clan stood like a choir and said in unison, "Happy Thanksgiving!"

A smile stretched from one side of my face to the other. "Happy Thanksgiving!"

Denise collected everyone's coats and, with Madison's help, carried them back to her bedroom. The decibels rose. When Tegan passed me, she placed a soft kiss on my lips and squeezed my arm. "Everything looks and smells great."

I whispered to Tegan, "How's your mom doing today?"

"The new drugs seem to be working. She's holding her own."

I kissed her cheek and followed her into the kitchen.

Everyone roamed through the house, talking about the flowers, the table setting, and how they liked its layout. Ashley returned from the patio. "Can we have a bonfire in your fire pit tonight?"

"Sure."

I overheard Denise describing the UD campus to Madison.

Beti walked around the dinner table and then headed to the counter. She held on to it and maneuvered around, stopping at each dish.

I bounced up and down on the balls of my feet. I leaned into Tegan. "Oh boy. She's inspecting the food, isn't she?"

Tegan smiled.

Beti lifted the aluminum covers, leaned down, and sniffed them, then replaced each one. When she returned the cover to the last dish, she looked up. "Dayna?"

My muscles tensed as I quickly came to her side.

She placed her hand on my forearm. "Everything looks and smells wonderful, and the table setting is beautiful," she said.

I couldn't hide my grin. "Thank you." All the tension left my body as Beti said she would like a glass of white wine.

Everyone got a drink and sat in the living room talking about the upcoming football game, the gifts the girls wanted for Christmas, and how we all wished for a cold winter but not a lot of snow.

"The smell of the food is making my stomach rumble," said Madison. "Can we eat now?"

I asked Nathan to bring the turkey and place it in front of him while everyone else grabbed a side dish. Liz filled the water glasses.

When everyone was seated, Beti asked, "Who is saying grace?"

Everyone turned to me. "Well." I turned to Tegan next to me and looked straight into her eyes. "Thanksgiving is a time to give thanks for the many blessings in our lives. One thing I'm thankful for is having met Tegan." I turned back to the table. "And having met all of you. I'm also thankful"—I looked at Denise—"that Denise and I have reconnected."

Denise nodded. "Me too."

"And thank you for all celebrating Thanksgiving in my home. Let's eat!"

Forty minutes later, there was another knock at the door, and Denise opened it to greet Marilyn, Stacy, Cindy, and Frieda. Raising two pies in her hands as Frieda lifted the ice cream, Stacy announced, "Dessert has arrived!"

Behind them were Leslie and Nedra. Nedra held another pie and said, "I hope you don't mind us crashing your party, but Leslie's parents got sick and had to cancel Thanksgiving dinner, and Marilyn and Stacy invited us to join them."

Tegan and I rushed to the door, and we had a group hug. "No problem. The more, the merrier. Come on in."

Denise and Madison collected their coats as Nathan and Phil squeezed six more chairs around the table.

Tegan did the introductions as Beti said, "Stacy, I remember you. You and Tegan were always getting into trouble together in high school."

Stacy hugged her. "Yep, that's me."

Phil said, "Long time no see."

Nathan pointed to Tegan and Stacy. "Could we tell you stories about these two?"

"Tell us, Dad," Ashley encouraged.

Stacy shook her finger and said to Phil and Nathan, "Don't you dare!"

Nathan and Phil crushed Stacy between them in a bear hug. When they released her, she said, "Well, I see hugging is still the Roberts' greeting."

Stacy grabbed Marilyn's hand. "This is my wife, Marilyn."

Liz said, "Good to meet you, and I hear congratulations are in order for your recent marriage," and hugged them both.

I placed clean plates, a pie cutter, and an ice cream scoop on the table, then stood back as they maneuvered for a seat, and finally, everyone sat shoulder to shoulder sardines-like. I chuckled as hands flew and mouths flapped. Beti smiled from ear to ear, holding hands with Ashley and Madison, who sat on either side of her. Frieda discussed college with Madison, and Cindy spoke with Ashley about boys. Leslie and Nedra discussed politics with Liz. Denise talked to Marilyn and Stacy about potential job opportunities while Phil and Nathan discussed the odds for the football game.

Tegan stood next to me. "Everything okay?"

I grabbed her hand. "There is so much goodness in this room. So much caring and love. Is this what it feels like to be part of a family?"

Her hand reached my cheek. "Yes."

"I know this is not the best time to say this, but I can't deny it to myself anymore."

Tegan tilted her head, and her eyes furrowed. "What?"

Over the clanging of spoons and people's conversations, I whispered in her ear, "I love you. And I promise..." I grabbed her hand in mine and placed it over her heart. "...to cherish and take care of your heart no matter what the future holds." Our clasped hands went to my chest. "You've captured my heart, body, and soul."

Tegan raised her hand to cover her mouth.

"I want to stay. Stay with you. Stay and be part of..." I waved my hand toward the chatter and laughter. "...all of this." I paused. "I want to stay by your side and show you every day, for as long as I live, how much I love you." Tears filled my eyes. "I want to stay."

Her expression was one of unwavering love and trust. In a soft voice, barely above a whisper, she said the four words that made my heart soar, "I love you too."

I met her halfway as she leaned in, hands cupping her face. Her cheeks were warm and smooth under my touch, and I could feel the gentle hum of energy flowing from her to me. Our lips met in a slow, comforting kiss that felt like coming home. It was as if a missing piece of my soul had been found.

As we turned, everyone's smiling faces and silence amplified our emotions. My heart raced as I lifted my glass and met Tegan's eyes. "Here's to family," I said softly. We turned with raised glasses as joyful cries of "To family" reverberated throughout the house.

Bella Books, Inc.
Happy Endings Live Here
P.O. Box 10543
Tallahassee, FL 32302
Phone: (850) 576-2370
www.BellaBooks.com

More Titles from Bella Books

Hunter's Revenge – Gerri Hill
978-1-64247-447-3 | 276 pgs | paperback: $18.95 | eBook: $9.99
Tori Hunter is back! Don't miss this final chapter in the acclaimed
Tori Hunter series.

Integrity – E. J. Noyes
978-1-64247-465-7 | 228 pgs | paperback: $19.95 | eBook: $9.99
It was supposed to be an ordinary workday...

The Order – TJ O'Shea
978-1-64247-378-0 | 396 pgs | paperback: $19.95 | eBook: $9.99
For two women the battle between new love and old loyalty may prove
more dangerous than the war they're trying to survive.

Under the Stars with You – Jaime Clevenger
978-1-64247-439-8 | 302 pgs | paperback: $19.95 | eBook: $9.99
Sometimes believing in love is the first step. And sometimes it's all
about trusting the stars.

The Missing Piece – Kat Jackson
978-1-64247-445-9 | 250 pgs | paperback: $18.95 | eBook: $9.99
Renee's world collides with possibility and the past, setting off a tidal
wave of changes she could have never predicted.

An Acquired Taste – Cheri Ritz
978-1-64247-462-6 | 206 pgs | paperback: $17.95 | eBook: $9.99
Can Elle and Ashley stand the heat in the *Celebrity Cook Off* kitchen?